# GRANTING HER WISH

USA TODAY BESTSELLING AUTHOR
## ERIN BEDFORD

# ALSO BY ERIN BEDFORD

### The Underground Series
Chasing Rabbits
Chasing Cats
Chasing Princes
Chasing Shadows
Chasing Hearts
The Crimes of Alice
Hatter's Heart

### The Mary Wiles Chronicles
Marked by Hell
Bound by Hell
Deceived by Hell
Tempted by Hell

### Starcrossed Dragons
Riding Lightning
Grinding Frost
Swallowing Fire
Pounding Earth

### The Crimson Fold
Until Midnight
Until Dawn
Until Sunset

### Curse of the Fairy Tales
Rapunzel Untamed
Rapunzel Unveiled
Rapunzel Unchained

<u>**Her Angels**</u>
Heaven's Embrace
Heaven's A Beach
Heaven's Most Wanted


<u>**House of Durand**</u>
Indebted to the Vampires
Wanted by the Vampires
Protected by the Vampires
Embrace of the Vampires
Tempted by the Butler
Loved by the Vampires
Huntress of the Vampires


<u>**Academy of Witches**</u>
Witching On A Star
As You Witch
Witch You Were Here
Just Witch It
Summer Witchin'


<u>**Children of the Fallen**</u>
Death In Her Eyes
Fire In Her Blood


**The Beast of the Fae Court**
**Granting Her Wish**
**Vampire CEO**

# CHAPTER 1
## *Alysha*

MY LIFE WASN'T SUPPOSED to be like this but when did anything ever go as planned for me? I can tell you, I'd never envisioned myself standing behind the register of Coffee and Stuff for the fifth year in a row. I'd thought I'd be out of this hell-hole by now. I'd thought I'd be running my own bakery, where someone would actually appreciate my hard work.

As I finished ringing the next customer up, I let out an aggravated sigh.

"That bad, Aly?"

My frown immediately turned upside down as my best friend, Jade Wiley, stepped behind the counter. Jade and I were a matched pair, dressed in identical uniforms that clashed with the dark blue Coffee and Stuff decor—black pants and an orange polo.

It was even worse for Jade, with her blonde hair dyed a two-toned mix of blue and purple—

which looked great with her complexion and her usual rocker attire. Not so much with our uniform.

"Worse." I gave her a knowing look and rolled my eyes. I pushed my burnt-coffee colored hair off my neck for the millionth time, wishing my mane wasn't so thick that regular hair ties couldn't contain it.

"Oh, yeah?" she asked as she handed the next order out and then took my place at the register. "Who are we dealing with today?"

"Hyde. Definitely Hyde."

Our boss, Bruce Thomas, and the owner of Coffee and Stuff, which should really be called 'Coffee and Shit', was the very definition of bipolar. Some days I'd come in, and he would be cheery as can be with compliments galore, but more often than not he'd be in a piss-poor mood and take it out on us. I chalked it up to his girlfriend not giving him any. The fact that the man even had a girlfriend was surprising at best. He was attractive enough, though. Nice hair, non-squinty eyes, and his nose and ears were proportionate to his face. But with the negativity flowing out of him, he could be a hotshot Hollywood actor, and he would still be one unattractive guy.

"What was your grievance this time?" Jade turned from her latest customer as I restocked the coffee. My lips twisted at her question. Most of the time I could brush off his insults and complaints. He'd say I'm late when I'm five minutes early, or the coffee was burnt when it was just the shitty coffee he bought. Today though . . . today was different.

"He insulted my muffins," I murmured, my eyes downcast.

"No!" Jade gasped, her hand going to her chest in horror. "I've had it." She untied the apron she had just put on, and threw it to the floor. "That wretched man has gone too far this time. I'm going to give him a piece of my mind."

I grabbed her arm before she could storm into the back and make a fool of herself. "Jade. It's fine. I'm fine. Don't lose your job because of me. You need it, remember?"

Jade and I both went to the same community college in Alinity, Kansas, for business and art respectively. She had been lucky enough to have parents who could afford to pay for her college. That was until they'd found out she wasn't going to be a lawyer like they'd wanted and then promptly cut her off. Now she was in the same boat as I was; dependent on student loans and this shitty-ass job. If she lost it, she'd have to drop out of school and go back home. I couldn't have that. She was the only thing keeping me going nowadays.

"But, Alysha . . . your muffins. Really?" The understanding in her eyes made my heart warm.

We both knew the only thing keeping this store from going under was the muffins I baked at home and brought in for us to sell.

I had brought them in one daya while ago—as a treat for Jade and me. Bruce had gotten a hold of a muffin on one of his good days and had offered me a raise if I'd continue to bring them in to sell at the shop.

Was it worth the extra fifty cents? Hell no. But I kept doing it because I loved to bake, and seeing the look on people's faces when they bit into something I'd made gave me a joy like nothing else ever has.

"It's fine, really." I waved her off and then sighed. "It's my fault anyway. He wanted blueberry today, and I brought chocolate chip. I shouldn't have deviated from the schedule."

Usually, when I baked, I created whatever inspired me that day. If I was having a bad day, I'd make a triple berry tart to brighten it up. If I was feeling frisky, I'd make a double chocolate devil's food cake. It was the same with my muffins.

Usually.

Bruce didn't like change though. He had made a schedule which I had unfortunately agreed to, and he expected me to adhere to it. Monday was supposed to be blueberry, and I had had the audacity to make chocolate chip which was only supposed to be served on Fridays.

"People don't like change," he'd said.

Well, those people can just go shove it.

"Just wait," Jade patted me on the shoulder, "Soon you'll get your own bakery, and we will both be out of this dump. Then you can make whatever you want, whenever you want."

"I hope so," I said and then frowned, "but that's not likely to happen if I can't get a loan from the bank to buy a shop. My savings can only get me so far and on the salary here? I'll be eighty before I can afford one on my own." I poured a cup of coffee and handed it to her for her customer.

My credit was not horrendous, but it wasn't great either. I used to have a crap ton of debt. Credit cards, car loans, you name it, I had it. But after my sleazebag ex—who'd convinced me to take on all that debt—and I had broken up, I'd paid the cards off, sold the car, and worked on getting my credit back up to where it was now.

But did banks care? No. They saw my past history of debt, a low-paying job, and student loans piling up to my ears. Which probably was something else going against me. I didn't know what it was about the older generation, but the moment they saw someone with more than just a single piercing in their ear, and—god forbid—a visible tattoo, they automatically put you in the 'irresponsible' column.

So I had a few piercings. Okay, maybe more than a few. The six on each ear would probably be pushing it for most people, but the stud in my nose and the bar through my tongue pretty much guaranteed me a spot on the young-people-these-days list. Hell, the one tattoo I did have was a teeny tiny fire Kanji behind my ear. I'd gotten it one night on a girl-power trip with Jade. She'd gotten a matching one on the inside of her wrist.

"Here you go, sir." Jade gave the customer a megawatt smile before turning back to me. "Don't worry, girl you'll get it. I can feel it."

I laugh-snorted at her words. Jade always had these feelings. Said she has a sixth sense of some kind, but, really, I think she uses it as a ploy to sell more paintings. People are dense and would buy anything they thought had magically appeared in her head. So far, she'd only gotten whack jobs wanting her otherworldly paintings.

Except for me, of course.

"You laugh now, but just wait. We'll be opening your shop in the next year, and then we'll see who will be laughing at who."

"Whom," I corrected her automatically, to which she responded with a death glare. I stuck my tongue out at her and then smiled.

A throat cleared behind me, and the smile on my face dropped. Ugh. Bruce.

"I see you girls are having fun." The very sound of his voice made all the happiness in the air sour, like condensed milk left out on the counter.

"We were." Jade couldn't seem to help herself as she turned from the counter to face our boss. The morning rush had died down, which meant Bruce was right on time to come harp on us. God forbid, the man actually did any real work.

"Well, if you girls have time for a chit-chat, then you have time to be cleaning. This place is a mess." He waved his hands around the pretty-much-spotless front area. As a baker, you'd think I would be the world's messiest person, but it just wasn't so. I hated dirty dishes and stained counters more than I hated pecan sandies. Which was saying something.

Jade and I exchanged a look and then in a mock salute, said in unison, "Aye aye, capt'n."

Picking up a wash rag I pretended to wipe away the nonexistent grime on the counter, but Bruce's voice stopped me. "Not you, Alysha."

"Huh?" I glanced over my shoulder at him.

He pointed a finger at Jade, and then me, then shook his head. "You two will do nothing but chit-chat if you're left alone together. You can go clean the back, while Jade handles the front."

"But what about the customers?" I gestured toward the cash register.

Bruce's lips twisted into a nasty smile. "I'm sure she can handle it. And if not . . . well . . . I shouldn't be paying her then anyway." Before either of us could get a word in edgewise, he moved around the counter and headed for the door.

"Where are you going?" Jade piped up, her hands on her hips. I could tell she was just about ready to explode with his attitude and after his thinly-veiled threat to fire her.

Pausing at the door, he narrowed his gaze at us. "I'm the boss here. Not you. I don't have to tell you anything. Now, get to work." He pointed at us once more before he darted out the door, leaving us as the only staffs in the shop.

Growling in frustration, Jade scrubbed at the counter furiously. I watched her for a moment or so. She wasn't going to be able to hold it in much longer. No more than thirty seconds later she tossed the rag down and spun around. "Who the hell does he think he is? Talking to us that way? We aren't children. We could run this shop better than he could, and on most days we do!"

"Shh," I tried to hush her, my eyes darting around to the customers who were oblivious to the wretchedness that was our boss, "Don't cause a scene. Just do your job and remember, we'll be out of here in a year, right?"

At the reference to her premonition, her scowl turned into a shit-eating grin. "You bet your sweet buns, we will be!"

I laughed at her idiom as I made my way to the back. I grabbed a bucket and filled it with soapy water. With a washrag tucked in my pocket, I considered what exactly I should clean.

There really wasn't much back here to tidy up. There was the stock room--which I didn't even want to get into—the refrigerator where we kept all the milk products, and then there was Bruce's office.

He never wanted us to go in there. Bruce always insisted that anything we needed to know he'd tell us. But with him out of the shop, and since he had told me to clean up the back, I felt justified in taking a peek inside.

The excitement to see what he had been hiding this whole time died the moment I turned on the light.

Boring. That was what it was. Utterly boring.

A second-hand desk and a line of file cabinets sat to one side. A mini fridge leaned against the wall, but even its contents were uninteresting. I had, at least, hoped to catch him drinking beer on the job, but alas there was only diet coke.

As I turned to leave his office, my joy in the unknown thoroughly squashed, I paused by the door and then took a step back as I caught sight of something. On the shelf above his desk sat a line of painted bottles. Those were something I would have never expected to see in his office. Bruce always made a point to comment about

Jade's career choice being a dead end, and of art being for the dull-minded.

*The little liar,* I thought, reaching up to pick up one of the bottles. Resembling a hookah, it had a long neck and a wide bottom. Blue and green stained glass decorated the outside, with a few gems dotted the surface here and there. The stopper seemed to be made out of real crystal, and when I tried to pop it from the top, it wouldn't budge.

Frowning at the bottle, I half wondered if Bruce stashed his weed in there. I remained so focused on the bottle I didn't hear Jade's voice until she was right outside the door. Startled, I jumped and the bottle fell from my hands into the bucket of water I'd left at my feet.

"Shit." I bent over to dig around in the bucket as Jade appeared in the doorway.

"He's coming back. What the hell are you doing in here?" She glanced around the office with disinterest.

"Cleaning, like he said." I grabbed hold of the neck of the bottle and lifted it from the bucket. Jade's eyes drew to it instantly. Excitement filled them but then disappeared as the front door's bell dinged. "Put that back before we both get fired."

She ducked out of the office, and I could hear her greet Bruce with a sickly-sweet voice. Not to look a gift horse in the mouth, I grabbed the rag out of my pocket and wiped the bottle off. My eyes darted to the door and back down to the bottle every few seconds expecting Bruce to walk in any minute.

The more I rubbed the surface, the warmer the bottle became until suddenly it began jumping around in my hands. Eyes wide, I fought to hold onto it, but it was like trying to keep a soufflé from sinking after it had already begun to fall. The bottle hopped out of my hands and landed on the floor with a clank that made me wince.

The stopper wiggled, the movement causing the bottle to rock back and forth. I held my hands out, each tilt made the need to grab it more intense. Eventually, the rocking stopped, and I inched toward it. The moment I touched the neck of the bottle the stopper popped out and landed on the floor.

Dark smoke billowed from the top. I coughed and waved my hand as I held the bottle away from me. What the hell did he have in this thing? A smoke bomb?

When the smoke cleared and I could breathe again, I bent down to grab the stopper off the floor but was stopped mid-bend by a foot that had appeared out of nowhere.

Encased in a black boot, the foot tapped steadily on the floor. My eyes followed the foot up along a pair of long legs covered by dark jeans, over a wide chest concealed in a tight black

shirt—that in any other situation would have
had me drooling—and then to the scowling face
of the man who had just appeared out of
nowhere.

# Chapter 2
## *Mac*

"WHO ARE YOU AND how did you get here?" were the first words out of my new master's mouth. No, 'thank you for coming' or 'I am forever grateful to you.' I swear humans became ruder by the century.

"You summoned me." I glared at her, crossing my arms over my chest as I looked my new master over.

She was a tiny little thing, with slender hips and chest just large enough to fill my hands. The outfit she wore didn't do her body justice. The colors washed out her skin and made her dark hair stand out even more.

Jewelry lined her ears, and as she spoke, something glinted inside her mouth. Was that a tongue piercing? Part of me wondered why someone would want such a thing, but the other part of me—a lower part that had no business tightening up at the sight—wanted to know what it would feel like against the underside of my cock.

I shook off the thoughts of my new master's luscious lips wrapping around my length and focused on the whole picture. She was vastly different from my previous masters, and I had no doubt she would be more than a handful. Especially since she was still yelling at me to leave.

Her eyes kept darting behind her, toward the sound of voices coming closer, but they were of no consequence to me. I only needed to grant wishes. Nothing more.

"I'm not leaving until you make your wishes," I said firmly, crossing my arms over my chest. "That's the rules, and I'd rather get this over and done with."

"Wishes?" She cocked her head to the side in an innocent way that made my lower region tighten even further.

*Stop it.* I growled at myself. Just because it had been a hundred years since I'd been with a woman didn't mean I should jump on the first one I saw.

"Yes, I am Mac'voniak, and you are my master until I grant you three wishes. Now," my gaze narrowed until my eyes were nothing more than slits, "what will they be?"

"Macvo-whoy whaty?" she attempted to say my name but gave up halfway. Shaking her head, she held her hands up. "Whatever your name is, I can't deal with this right now. My boss will be here any second and I cannot get fired, so just . . ." my new master picked up my bottle and shoved it at me, "get back in or whatever."

I stared down at the bottle with disdain. I'd just gotten out of that damned prison, no way was I getting back in anytime soon. Master or not.

When I made no move to get back into my bottle, she let out an aggravated groan. Grabbing hold of my arm, she held the bottle in her other hand and attempted to drag me out of the room. Not wanting to make it easy for her, I dug my feet into the ground and glared.

"I told you, I'm not leaving until I grant your wishes." This time I put a growl in my voice hoping to intimidate her into complying.

"Give me a break!" Letting out a growl of her own, she placed her hands on her hips—awkwardly since she still held my bottle-prison in her hand. "Look if you want to get caught fine, but I'm out of here. I might hate this job, but I still need it."

To my utter horror, after saying her piece, she flung my bottle at me. I barely caught it before it hit the ground. My new master stomped from the room, leaving me holding the bottle and staring down at my prison with a mixture of fear and abhorrence. To think what could have happened if this thing had shattered? I shuddered at the thought then tucked it under my arm.

Jaw clenched, a sickening knot in my stomach formed as the pull of my master getting further away from me activated the bond between us. *Oh, how I hated it.*

A stranger stepped into the room, and I instinctively dematerialized. His eyes widened and he shook his head, but before he could register what he was seeing, I was gone.

I reformed in a bigger room than the first, this one full of people who didn't even notice as I appeared out of thin air. But my new master did, though.

My—as yet nameless—master, rushed around the counter where she had been standing with another female. My brow lifted at her companion's unnatural hair color, which I could only assume was self-inflicted. Unlike my new master, her gaze roamed over my form, and when she licked her lips in appreciation, I couldn't help but smirk.

Women, especially, human women, had always found me attractive. While I didn't often lower my standards to mess with humans, on occasion—when the loneliness of being exiled from my own kind got to be too much for me—I would indulge in a human woman or two. They usually left satisfied, if not besotted with me.

Except for one human. My eyes locked onto my new master, who now stopped before me. Hands on her hips once more, she glared up at me.

"What the hell do you think you're doing?" she snapped at me, her eyes flashing with annoyance before they searched around the room. No doubt to make sure no one had seen my sudden appearance. "You can't just do that here."

I shrugged. "What are you going to do about it?"

Gnashing her teeth, she stomped a foot before shoving a finger at a table near us. "Go sit over there until my shift was over. Then I'll deal with you later."

"Not until I tell you the rules." I planted my feet firmly in place, about to tell my new master the usual spiel that I am bound by law to tell her, but she cut me off.

"I get three wishes. I got it." She rolled her dark eyes at me and then a voice from behind the counter made her turn around. She suddenly called out, "I'm with a customer!"

"There's more to it than that," I said before she could take off on me again, "And I am duty bound to tell you."

"Fine!" she snapped, her eyes jerking back to me. "Say what you have to say so I can get back to work." My master bounced in place and pointed a thumb back to the counter.

The man in the other room who had almost seen me came to mind. Was that her boss? Why was she so afraid of such a puny man?

I shook off the thoughts. Not my problem. I was just here to do my job, and that was all. Maybe this would be the final master, and maybe she would give me my freedom. Even as I thought it I knew the probability was highly unlikely.

*As if they'd be so kind.*

"Rule one," I began. "This one should be obvious. You get three wishes, and you can't wish for more wishes."

"Fine. Good," she interrupted me again causing me to scowl.

"Rule two, no speaking when I'm speaking."

"That's not a rule. You just made that up," she accused me with a pointed finger.

"No, it's a rule." I *had* just made it up, but she didn't need to know that. She opened her mouth to interject again, so I quickly added, "Rule three, wording is everything. If you are not specific in your request, then do not blame me when it doesn't come out the way you planned it."

"That's hardly fair." The woman's lips pressed into a thin line. "How am I supposed to know what you will twist around?"

I smirked. "Not my problem."

Seeing I wasn't going to move on this, she nodded. "Fine. Is that it?"

I shook my head. "No, there's a few more disclosures that we must discuss." Before I could tell her, the purple-and-blue haired woman at the counter, leaned over and hissed.

"Aly, he's coming!"

*Aly?*

My new master turned to the girl and then back to me. "We'll talk about them later. Go sit over there." She pointed at the table again before hurrying back to the counter just in time to meet the man I saw from before.

"Where have you been?" The man glowered at her, and I frowned as my new master stumbled over her words as she tried to explain what had happened. An unusual need to step in and help her threatened to overwhelm me, but I shoved it back down where it belonged.

The older man reamed into her for a few more minutes, and she simply stood there and took it. Seeing her let him talk to her that way, left a bad taste in my mouth. I didn't care for bullies, but even less so for those who let others walk all over them. And my new master seemed to be one of the latter.

The man finally left her, disappearing into the back room once more. My new master, Aly—I assumed from what the other woman had called her—made a rude gesture as soon as his back was turned. That made me smile. She might not be such a pushover after all.

I took a seat at the table Aly had indicated watched my master with new interest. She had no problem yelling at someone she didn't even know, but for some reason, she cared enough about her job that she clearly hated to not stand up for herself against her boss. A complex mystery she was. One I wouldn't mind unraveling.

I shook the thought away before my mind could head in the wrong direction once more. I really needed to find some relief; it had been too long. The last thing I wanted, or needed, was to become too attached to my master. Once this job was done, I was out of here and hopefully back to where I belonged.

On my throne.

# CHAPTER 3
## *Alysha*

BRUCE WAS A REAL piece of work. Not only had he disappeared on us for over an hour, but then he'd returned and demanded to know why I'd cleaned the back. Really? Come on. He'd flat out asked me to. What the hell had he expected me to do?

I'd stood there while he'd berated me—silently trying not to punch him in the face like he deserved—while at the same time fighting with myself not to look at the sex-god who had suddenly come into my life. Now, with Bruce hiding away in his office, as usual, I could check on my supposed genie in peace.

He didn't say he *was* a genie, but three wishes and emerging from a bottle? All the evidence pointed to the only logical answer. He was a genie. My genie, for that matter.

Inwardly, I did a little dance of excitement. *I had a genie. I had a genie.* Then panic flowed in.

*I had a genie!* What the hell was I going to do with a genie? And then there were the rules he'd been trying to tell me about.

Suddenly, all the different horrible scenarios that could happen from making the wrong wish filled my mind. I'd heard about wishes gone wrong. Not in real life—god no—but in movies and such. You wish for a million dollars, and your favorite relative dies, leaving you the money. Or you want to get out of work, and so you end up in a coma.

Neither of those scenarios were something I wanted. I didn't even want the genie for that matter. Right now, I had my life going the direction I wanted—except for the loan part—but that would take time and hard work, not some magic wish.

No. He'd have to go back to where he'd come from.

Mind made up, I turned to tell him just that when Jade moved into my line of sight.

"Man, what is his problem?" she sneered toward the direction Bruce had gone.

"The usual." I shrugged and tried to nonchalantly move around her so that Macov-what's-his-name was in my view. He sat there in all his yummy goodness, one leg crossed over the other, his hand tapping away on the surface of the table. The bottle—*his* bottle—sat in front of him.

God, I hoped Bruce didn't notice it was missing. The thought made me wonder why he'd even had a genie-bottle in the first place? Had my boss known he had a genie in his possession?

No, I decided immediately. If he did know, I didn't doubt he would have used the genie by now to get his girlfriend to marry him.

An elbow shoved into my side and jolted me out of my thoughts. I rubbed my ribs and glared at Jade who frowning at me.

"What?" The word came out a bit more forceful than I'd meant it to be.

"What's up with you?" My best friend tilted her head to the side. "Usually, after the boss-man drills into you like that you can't wait to bitch about him, but here you are, lost in thought." Her brows rose and her mouth curved into a knowing grin. "I bet it has to do with the hottie over there eyeballing you."

Jade twisted around and waved at him, giving him a flirty wink. I grabbed her by the shoulders and pulled her back to me.

"What the hell are you doing?" I scowled.

Jade shrugged. "Just saying 'hello' to your friend. Unless he's your boyfriend now?"

"No." Releasing her, I snatched a rag off the counter and started cleaning the spotless surface vigorously.

"Why not?" She leaned her hips against the counter right next to where I was scrubbing.

"He's attractive, you're attractive. You could be attractive together. And God knows you are wound tighter than a nun's habit."

"Jade!" My eyes shot to the guy in question, hoping he had been a figment of my over-caffeinated imagination. But alas, he was still there, smirking as if he knew we were talking about him. Which, in the tiny coffee shop, I had little doubt he did.

"He's not my anything." I threw the rag down on the counter and turned to my best friend. "If you want him, go for it. I won't stop you." Even as I told her I wasn't interested, a part of me screamed for me to shut up.

But I pushed it aside. I didn't know this guy. I'd just met him. There was nothing saying I had dibs on him or whatnot. *But he did say you were his master. Wasn't that calling dibs?* I bit my cheek in an attempt to calm my warring mind.

"Really?" Jade asked from beside me, her gaze shifting to where he sat. "You wouldn't mind? 'Cause I could use a hot guy like that. I've dated too many artists lately, and that guy does not look like an artist."

Her comment made me pause. "What makes you say that?"

"Just look at him," Jade said, gesturing toward him. "Those muscles, that jawline, his hands. Pick a feature!" She shook her head, desire clear in her eyes. "That is not a prissy hormonal artist. That's a man who likes to get down and dirty. Someone who can take a hit and give one in return. You know . . . a real man's man."

I almost laughed at her description, but it pulled on something low in me. Licking my lips, I couldn't help but imagine him working underneath the hood of a car, his shirt off, skin glistening in the sun. He wouldn't be too distracted by his own work to stop and throw me over whatever he was working on to have his way with me. A slight shiver ran through me at the thought.

"Anyways," Jade puffed her hair and then adjusted her boobs in her top, "Wish me luck!"

Reluctantly, I watched as she made her way around the counter and stopped in front of my genie. My genie? When had he become mine?

Not having an answer, I focused on trying to hear their conversation.

"Hey, there," Jade purred, really laying it on. She placed one hand on the table and leaned slightly toward him so that her chest—much bigger than mine—was right in his line of sight. From where I stood, I couldn't tell his expression, and part of me wasn't sure I wanted to.

"Hello," he answered in a deep voice in which—now that I wasn't panicking about Bruce—I could sense a hint of an accent. I couldn't tell where it was from, but it sounded exotic, which only added to his appeal.

"I saw you over here all by yourself and wanted to see if I could get you anything," Jade asked in a coy voice. "Anything at all."

"I'd like to talk to your friend over there," he said in a cool tone causing Jade's seductive pose to dissipate.

She glanced over her shoulder at me, not at all bothered that he asked for me instead of her. Giving me a told-you-so look, she turned back to him. "Sure, I'll get her."

Frowning at my friend, but inwardly a bit happy the genie had turned her down, I waited for her to come back to the counter. The genie's eyes stayed on me and I found myself locked in a staring contest I couldn't get out of. There was something about him, something which made me possessive, but at the same time, I wanted him as far away from me as possible. He was trouble, I could tell, and I'd had my share of trouble. I wanted simple. Honest. Not spine-tingling smiles and empty promises. I'd had enough of those with my ex.

It wasn't until Jade stopped at my side that I jerked away from the genie's gaze.

"So," she said with a raised brow.

"So what?" I turned away from her prying eyes and started restocking the counter.

"He asked for you. Aren't you going to go over there?" The tone of her voice told me clearly what she thought I should do. Which I had no intention of doing.

"No. I'm working."

"So? You get a break." Jade snatched the box of straws I had just taken out and held it above her head.

"Give it back, Jade." I held my hand out and tried not to scowl. She was such a child sometimes.

"Not until you agree to go talk to tall-dark-and-yummy over there." She gestured with her head toward my mysterious visitor.

Brows scrunching together, I contemplated the likelihood that she would leave me in peace, but I suspected she would torment me for the rest of our shift until I did as she wanted. Finally giving up, I sighed and reached back to untie my apron.

Jade let out a little squeal and clapped her hands. "Okay, let's fix your hair first." She reached over to adjust my hair but stopped at Bruce's annoyed voice.

"What do you think you are doing?" he growled. "This isn't beauty class. We aren't at a sleepover. You are at work, and touching your hair is unsanitary."

Before Jade could jump in and get us both in trouble, I stepped in front of her, "I was just about to go on break, Bruce. Jade was just helping me get my apron off."

"No, you aren't," Bruce snapped. "We need more dark roast, and all those napkin holders need to be filled. As far as I can tell you haven't done anything but chitchat on my dime." His lips twisted into a snarl. "Get back to work. And if I catch you two gossiping again, I'll make sure your shifts never coincide with each other again."

Stomping away, he left me boiling. Usually, I could just brush off his remarks, but yelling at us for no reason and then saying I hadn't earned my break? I worked harder than *he* did and it was his freaking shop.

"Ugh!" I curled my fingers in front of me, imagining it was Bruce's neck there for me to strangle. "Just ugh!"

"You said it, girl." Jade nodded. "He's so full of shit. I have half a mind to key his car. In fact," she half jumped in place, "I think I will do just that!"

Ignoring my best friend's proclamation, I ground my teeth together. "He's such an asshole."

"Preach!" Jade held her hand up, egging me on.

"He's just so...ugh." He made me so mad, I couldn't even get the words out. "Every day I come in here and work like a dog for him, and not once has he said 'thank you'. Or even been nice to me!"

"Uh-huh. Totally unacceptable." She crossed her arms over her chest and glared at the door Bruce had left through.

"I just wish..." my fingers curled into fists and tightened until the nails bit into my palms, "I just wish he would break a leg or something so he would give us a freaking break!"

The moment the words left my mouth I wished I could take them back. The world seemed to slow around me as I turned and searched out my genie. The whole time I hoped against hope that he hadn't heard me. But when I saw the look on the genie's face—a triumphant smile that made my blood freeze—I knew there was no such luck.

He didn't wrinkle his nose or bob his head. He made no indication at all that he had done something. A hopeful part of me wondered if he had been full of shit after all. When a crash came from the back, followed by Bruce's yell, that thought was firmly destroyed.

Shooting a scathing glare at the genie—who simply smiled at me— I raced to Bruce's office, Jade close behind me.

Bruce was lying on the ground, groaning and holding his leg, a mess of papers scattered around him. The metal file cabinet, which usually stood by his desk, now rested on its side next to a ladder which had certainly not been there before.

"What happened?" I asked, my anger gone and worry taking its place. I kneeled by his side, my eyes scanning him to see if he had quite literally broken his leg.

"I tripped over this damn ladder." Bruce shoved a hand at the ladder and then groaned again grabbing at his leg. "When did we even get this thing?"

"I don't know." I shook my head, exchanging a look with Jade who seemed as perplexed as I was. "Just stay here. I'll call an ambulance."

Leaving Jade to stay at Bruce's side, I stomped out of the office and toward the front, eyes landing on the genie who had gotten up from his seat. He stood by the counter, his hands in his tight pants as he rocked on his heels.

"Believe me now?"

He quirked a brow at me, and I scowled. "You, come with me."

# CHAPTER 4
## *Mac*

THE WAY HER BOSS treated her I would think she'd be happy to get rid of him. She'd wished for him to break his leg. I had only done what she'd wished for. I'd told her to be careful, but she hadn't listened.

*They never did.*

After Aly called someone to come help her boss, she grabbed me by the arm and dragged me out of the shop. This time I didn't fight her. I allowed her pull me out the front doors and down the sidewalk.

"What is your problem?" she snarled at me in a hushed tone, which didn't keep other humans on the sidewalk from glancing our way curiously as they passed.

"I don't know what you mean," I answered, scratching my ear. I hoped my body language told her how much I didn't want to be there. Or how much I didn't care about her problems.

Crossing her arms over her chest, she tapped her foot in an irritated rhythm. "Don't play dumb with me. You know exactly what I mean."

"I'm just doing my job. You wish it, I fulfill it. Not my fault you can't handle the consequences." I shrugged before slightly turning from her as a busty woman brushed by me. My eyes trailed after her for a moment, watching the swish of her skirt which barely covered her backside.

"Hello!" Aly's fingers snapped in front of my face, and I turned my attention back to her. Her eyes darted behind me, and her frown deepened. "Genie or not you're such a guy."

"I never said I wasn't." My brows furrowed not sure where she was going with her line of thought. "So, are you going to make your other two wishes so I can get out of here?"

She gave me an incredulous stare before forcefully snapping, "No!"

"No need to shout. I'm just doing my job."

"So, your job includes ruining people's lives?" Aly said, utter disgust dripping from her words. Not that I cared what she thought of me. All I cared about was getting this job over with and getting back to my kingdom where I belonged.

"No. You—humans—do that well enough all on your own." I couldn't help but smirk.

"That's beside the point. I didn't mean for you to actually break his leg!" She threw her hands up in the air. "I didn't mean to wish anything at all."

"I told you before. I'm not responsible for your wishes going wrong," I shrugged with indifference, "You should be more careful."

Aly grabbed her head with her hands and closed her eyes briefly. A slight rumble came from her. My master was quite an interesting specimen, I'd give her that. Though, so far, she had been exactly like the others. Not taking it seriously and then blaming me for their problems.

"Look," she said after a moment, letting go of her head and locking eyes with me. Her eyes, a color so dark they almost enveloped her pupils, filled with irritation and exhaustion. "I don't have time to mess with you right now. I have a job to try and keep, and with Bruce gone, I'll be the one who has to close the shop now. So thank you for that."

The sarcasm in her voice wasn't lost on me, but I didn't comment on it. Instead, I angled my head to the side and asked, "What do you wish me to do?" I glanced around the area she had brought us to. The shop sat on the corner of a somewhat-busy street. There were a few vehicles passing every few moments, but pedestrians constantly flowed past on the sidewalk. The gray concrete and metal was a far cry from my world.

In Tavokia, the cities were colorful and lively. Everyone knew everyone, and not a person went by without being greeted. Even a crown prince, like myself, would be stopped on the street to chat about the recent developments in the kingdom. Not that I would have walked amongst the peasants in such a manner.

Inwardly, I scoffed at the thought and then chastised myself. That kind of thinking was what had gotten me into this situation in the first place.

Thinking of my home made my heart sink, and I frowned. I hadn't been back to Tavokia in centuries, I didn't even know if it still looked the way it had when I'd left. Or even if it was still there at all. No doubt my cousin had taken up the throne and had run the kingdom into ruin.

"Are you listening to me?"

Jerking out of my thoughts, I looked down at my new master with a grim expression. "Not really."

"Ugh!" She stomped her little foot and pointed a finger at me. "You're impossible. Just stay away from the shop alright? I'll meet you after work."

My brows furrowed at her demands. "You expect me to just wait around for you? I'm not a slave."

This time she smirked at me. "Genie, remember? You're supposed to be listening to me."

"No, I'm supposed to grant your wishes. There is no rule about me obeying your every command. In fact, I refuse." I crossed my arms over my chest defiantly.

After my little announcement, I'd have expected her to throw a fit, or just give in to my demands so I could get away from this god-forsaken place. What I hadn't expected was for her to come incredibly close to me, her hand curling into the front of my shirt as she jerked me down to her eye level. Surprise filled me, but I didn't pull away.

"You might think you are better than us humans. But here, buddy, you are at my command. Do what I say or I'll never ever make my other two wishes, and you'll be stuck here until I die," her jaw clenched as she gave me a nasty smile, "And believe me when I say I'm stubborn enough to hold on for eons."

I heard what she was saying, but for some reason, all I could think about was the intoxicating smell which filled my nose. A sweet buttery scent pulled on parts of me that hadn't been awake in years. Suddenly, the prospect of being by her side for decades didn't seem unappealing. It might even be refreshing to be with one person for an indefinite amount of time.

I shook the thought from my head. I couldn't stay here with her. I hardly knew the woman, and there was the matter of getting my kingdom back that needed to be addressed.

So instead of taking hold of my new master the way my body was urging me to do, I leaned down until my mouth was almost brushing hers. Her body tensed at my sudden closeness, and I resisted the urge to press my form against hers to see if her curves were really as soft as they looked.

"Try me," I whispered my words so close to her face it caused the reaction I'd hoped for.

A gasp fell from her lips, and her breath caught. She licked her lips, and my eyes shot down to follow the movement. Aly might play the tough-as-nails card, but she was still a woman. One who was very much affected by me.

"Uh..." For once she seemed lost for words, her hands still held out in front of her as if she didn't know what to do with them. Aly's dark gaze darted to my face and then down to my lips before they shot back up again. Suddenly, as if burned, she stumbled away from me and pointed toward the shop.

"I have to get back to work." She moved past me quickly, being careful not to touch me. It made the smile on my lips spread even further.

"What do you wish me to do, Master?" I called after her. She paused and turned back to me.

Her eyes wouldn't meet mine but seemed to be focused on the ground in front of me. "I don't care. Just stay out of the shop. I'll be off at ten."

Her words came out rushed as if she couldn't stand to be in my presence for a second longer. And the moment they were out of her mouth she spun on her heel and headed back into the shop, letting the door slam shut behind her.

My lips pressed into a thin line. Curious. My new master had all kinds of sides to her. First, there was her no-nonsense I-don't-have-time-for-anyone-but-work part. Then her boss had gotten onto her. She had easily been subjugated, but afterward, she'd let her displeasure of the man be known, leading to her first wish.

Her anger at my granting the wish wasn't surprising. Most of my previous masters rarely meant their first wish, but none of them had blatantly refused to make their other two wishes. They had just been more careful about how they'd worded it and then had made them quickly to get rid of me.

My usual approach wasn't going to work on Aly. Though, the way she had reacted just now did have promise. If I couldn't intimidate her into making her wishes, I could always seduce her into doing it.

If anyone was paying any mind to me standing in the middle of the sidewalk they'd have said the expression on my face was positively wicked.

With a plan in mind, I relaxed a bit and took in my surroundings.

The world hadn't changed much in the time since I'd had my last master. I'd have to say it's only been a decade, if that. The cars were a bit updated and the clothing . . . my eyes found another attractive woman wearing little more than a t-shirt and heels. I had to say I didn't have a problem with what humans called fashion nowadays. They sure made things more bearable.

Much better than being inside of my bottle. Which, I realized in a panic, still sat on the table in the shop. I hurried to the shop window, my heart beating rapidly in my chest. When I saw Ally had put the bottle behind the counter where she stood, I let out a heavy sigh.

That could have been bad.

As much as I hated the bottle, I was bound to it. If it broke, I wouldn't die so much as lose all my abilities. Which meant I would be stuck in the human world. The very thought of it made me shudder.

While the human world might have some appeal to others of my kind, I'd never been one to care for it. I'd been on the way to making it illegal to even visit this world before I was sentenced to my tiny prison.

"You need to learn humility, Mac'voniak," I could still hear my father's voice say in my ear before he cast the spell binding me to the bottle. The look of regret on his face had done nothing to dampen the scorching betrayal I'd felt.

Now, after a thousand years of servitude, I didn't hate him anymore. I understood why he had done it. I had been a petulant child who'd thought he knew everything. In some ways, I was still that same child, but I hoped in the time I'd served the humans I'd proven myself worthy of the Tavokian throne.

I'd been lucky to catch another one of my kind around my third master. A lower-class Tavokian, but one of my kind nonetheless. He'd worn a solemn expression as he had informed me that my father had fallen ill shortly after I had left and my cousin, Ga'nova, ruled in my stead.

The thought of my cousin on my throne caused a whole other kind of anger. I was mad at myself for getting stuck here, and I resented my cousin for taking what should be mine. And the longer I stayed on earth, the less likely it was that I would ever be getting home.

I glanced at my new master who had plastered on a smile which actually looked genuine as she served customers. Something twanged inside of me at her smile. I promptly squashed it with a shake of my head. I didn't have time to be distracted.

*Seduce the human. Grant the wishes. Get home.*

With my plan plainly laid out inside of my head, I searched for somewhere to wait until the shop closed. I wasn't letting Aly out of my sight for a moment. Who knew when the next chance to grant her wish might come up?

# CHAPTER 5
## *Alysha*

THE DAY WENT ON with no more incidents. Bruce had been taken to the hospital where they had confirmed he had indeed broken his leg. Which meant I had to take over closing up the shop and opening it again the next morning. I'd tried to explain to Bruce I had class in the morning and didn't have time to open the shop for the morning shift, but he was having none of it.

"Either be there or don't come back in again," he'd snarled into the phone, his words pretty slurred since he was so heavily medicated. I doubt he would even remember our conversation let alone be able to fire me. But I couldn't take the chance. I needed this job, at least for a little while more.

I sighed again for the millionth time. Could today get any worse? *No, don't say that.* It could very well get worse.

"Is he just going to sit there all night?" Jade asked me, leaning against the mop she had been using on the floor.

My eyes shot to where Mac—as I had begun to refer to him in my head—sat on a bench across the street. Ever since I had come back into the shop, there'd been a tight knot between my shoulder blades. I couldn't seem to relax as long as my new friend was around. I'd gone through the motions of making coffee and taking orders through the lunch rush, and then grudgingly through the dinner rush. Luckily, I had Jade by my side the whole time, or I wouldn't have been able to make it through the day.

*Double shifts were a bitch.*

Mac sat on the bench the entire time. Every once in a while, he would adjust his position, but for the most part, his eyes were locked on me. I flushed at the intensity of his gaze.

His hot and cold personality gave me whiplash of epic proportion. While I didn't trust his sudden interest, a part of me still enjoyed it. But no matter his attractiveness, or his sudden interest in me, he clearly didn't care for humans and wouldn't be caught dead with one.

"Probably," I muttered to myself as I finished counting up the till. While tired, I didn't hurry to get the job done since after work I would have to deal with Mac and everything that came with him.

*Two more wishes,* I mused. What would I do with two wishes? I would have had three had I not wasted the first one on my damnable boss. But it was better that I only had the two in the long run. Less chance Mac would twist my words around and hurt someone else.

"Hey, Jade." I paused in my counting for a moment.

"Yeah?" She angled her head to me to show me she was listening while resuming the mopping.

"If you had three wishes what would you wish for?"

Jade stopped mopping and turned around to face me. There was a pensive look on her face as she thought about my question. "I guess . . . to become a famous artist." She shrugged. "There's not much else I want," Jade stopped and then smiled, "Well, except maybe a double cheeseburger with loaded French fries!"

I laughed with her before going back to counting. Well, she wasn't helpful.

I marked down the count, making a note of any discrepancies before putting it in the bag Bruce used for overnight drops. Of course, since he was in the hospital it was up to me to make the drop tonight, or do it in the morning before I went to class. Since I wasn't going to have enough time to eat, let alone go to the bank, I had to do it tonight.

"Are you about done?" I asked Jade as I got my stuff together to head out the door.

Seeing me grab my bag, Jade promptly dropped the mop back into the bucket and shoved it behind the counter. "I am now."

I knew for a fact she'd only mopped about one fraction of the floor of the shop, but I didn't mention it. Jade was probably just as worn out as I was.

"Do you want me to come with you?" Jade nodded to the deposit bag in my hand as she put the strap of her bag over her head.

I thought about it for a moment but then remembered who was waiting for me on the bench outside. "No, I've got it. You go on home."

Her eyes glanced behind me, and she gave me a knowing grin before winking. "You got it, Al."

We walked around the counter and through the front door, flipping the lights off as we went. I locked the front door and pulled the metal security gate that slid down over it, locking it as well.

"You know," Jade drew out, "any guy that determined at least deserves a good squeeze of the girls." She grabbed at her chest mockingly.

"Jade!" I scowled. "I hardly know the guy. He's not squeezing anything."

Shrugging a shoulder, Jade said, "Your loss. I'd happily offer up my own melons, but I don't think he'd be interested. Anyways," she looked down at her phone as she typed something before shoving it into her pocket, "I've got to meet Gregory. He's been drinking too much again and needs me to talk him down."

"Going to burn all his stuff again, huh?" Gregory was Jade's on-again-off-again boyfriend, who just didn't know when to take a break. He was constantly drinking or smoking pot which lead to self-pity. Gregory threatened to destroy all of his work at least once a month, which Jade and I knew he would regret the next day.

"Yeah, so my night is pretty much a bust." She frowned and then smirked at me. "So, you'll have to give me all the gory details tomorrow about Mr. Hottie."

Jade pointed a thumb back at Mac who had risen from his spot across the street and was now heading our way. Not answering her, I watched him approach. While his clothing wasn't impressive—other than the way they seemed to wrap around every muscle deliciously—there was something distinctive about the way he moved. Head held high, his steps were precise and so sure of themselves as if he was walking on the red carpet and not the dirty street.

"Finally," Mac said as he approached us. "Do all humans work this late?"

Ignoring the questioning look Jade had at his wording, I jumped in, "Some work even later. All night even. So no complaining."

Jade stared at us, obviously trying to figure out our dynamic. If I was dating anyone new, she would know, and Mac's sudden appearance was suspicious. Inhumanly so.

Before my best friend could start asking questions I didn't want to answer, I gestured to her. "I forgot to introduce you. Jade, this is Mac. Mac, my best friend, Jade."

Mac gave me a curious look but didn't question my nickname for him. If I tried saying his long-ass name to Jade, I'd have looked even more suspicious.

"Hi." Jade accepted my introduction and offered him a hand. He glanced down at it as if she had handed him something from the trash bin. Reluctantly, he took her hand in his and shook it.

There was obvious tension between the two of us that Jade, thankfully, was smart enough to pick up on. "Well, Gregory's waiting for me. So, I'll just let you two get on with it."

As she left, Jade made a lewd gesture behind Mac's back which I repaid with a warning glare. She returned my glare with a smile and then headed down the street, leaving me utterly alone with my hunky salivation-worthy problem.

"So," Mac clapped his hands together, completely obvious to what had just transpired behind his back as he rubbed them together, "are you ready to make your two wishes?"

"Is that all you ever think about?" I rolled my eyes and started down the street. I had tucked the bank bag into my purse, so it didn't look as appealing to thieves. I clutched my bag close to me, my eyes open for any suspicious characters.

"Yes," he stated plainly as he followed beside me. His legs were longer than mine, so he had to take smaller steps, which made me smile.

"Don't you do anything else? Have hobbies? A girlfriend?" Okay, so that last part was me being nosy, but seriously, the guy needed a different focus.

He was quiet for a moment and then answered, "When you are forced into servitude like I have been, you don't really have time for hobbies. Though, I have had many lovers over the centuries."

"Oh," I said. Disappointment filled me. I shouldn't be surprised. He was a hot guy. Of course, he'd have lovers. Probably more than one at a time. While I was just a lowly human who couldn't even get a loan for her dream shop.

"But I haven't found anyone who truly interests me," he continued, giving me a sideways grin.

"Oh!" I said with a little too much enthusiasm.

He nodded slightly. "When you have lived hundreds of years like myself it's easy to get bored. Though, I have to say I enjoy this century's clothing much more than the previous one."

My brows furrowed at what he'd said. Hundreds of years old? I liked older men, but hundreds of years was kind of pushing it.

Trying not to let what he said bother me, I asked, "So how many masters have you had?"

He seemed to think about it for a moment before answering, his voice unsure, "About a hundred and fifty-four, you would be a hundred and fifty-five."

"Wow," I couldn't help but say, "That's a lot of wishes."

Mac nodded again and then tucked his hands in his pockets. "I was passed around from master to master for a few years back in the Middle Ages. That's where the bulk of my masters came from. Which was probably why they ended up calling them the dark ages." He chuckled, a sound that reverberated through me and settled low inside of me.

*Oh, boy.*

I didn't have a chance to chastise myself for my heightened libido because we had arrived at the bank drop off. I used the key to open the box and then quickly looked around for anyone unruly before I grabbed the bank bag from my purse and shoved it in the drawer.

"Does your employer usually leave such dangerous tasks to women?" Mac asked, a disapproving expression on his face.

I shrugged. "Not usually, he's too much of a penny-pincher to let any of us handle the money, but he didn't have much choice today since he broke his leg." I shot him a look, and he didn't even bother trying to look contrite.

"So where to next? To your home?"

I thought about it. I didn't know this guy. Did I really want him in my apartment? There was no telling what he could, or would, do. On the other hand, I couldn't very well put him up in a hotel. Lack of funds for one thing. For another, it didn't feel right since I was supposedly his master.

Sighing, I pointed down the street. "Come on, I live down that way. We have quite a walk ahead of us."

"Why do you not have a vehicle?" His gaze shifted to one of the few cars that passed by.

"Because," I started walking, expecting him to follow me, "Cars are expensive, and my job isn't that far. And I could use the exercise."

I didn't like having to explain my situation to him. I didn't add the part about not being able to afford a car or even get a loan because of my dead-beat ex-boyfriend. That was a bit too personal for someone I'd just met.

We walked down the street in a slightly awkward silence. When we finally reached my apartment, I led him through the rickety security-door that really didn't do much to keep people out, and then up the stairs. I lived on the fifth floor, and we didn't have an elevator, so once more I did it for the exercise. Or I kept telling myself that.

When we got to my apartment, number 5A, I prepared to unlock the door, but then paused and turned to him. "Look, I'm just a college student with a minimum wage job. So, my home isn't anything extravagant. So, there's nothing for you to break or steal."

I wished I had kept my mouth shut because the look Mac gave me could only be described as scathing.

He took a step toward me forcing me to move away, but when the door pressed against my back, I ran out of room. Placing one hand on either side of me, he leaned down until we are inches apart. This was the second time today we had been so close together, and it had an even more profound effect on me now than it had in the middle of the sidewalk.

"Human," he growled, "I am a prince amongst my people. I do not need, nor do I want, your belongings. I only want for you to make your wishes so I can go."

Swallowing thickly, I licked my lips. "Alright, got it."

When he stepped away from me, I let out a
breath I hadn't realized I'd been holding. Turning
from him, I shoved the key in the door and
pushed it open. This was going to be a long night.

# CHAPTER 6

## *Mac*

STAYING WITH ALY WAS very different than my previous masters. Most hadn't even bothered to invite me to their home; they just assumed I'd show up when they needed me. Like some kind of spiritual being.

Pfft. I was a genie. Not some all-powerful being. If I had been, I'd be able to get myself out of here and back home whenever I wanted.

"I only have my bedroom," Aly told me, her posture unsure as her eyes darted around the room, "So, I hope the couch is alright? Or do you sleep in your bottle?"

She pulled my prison for the last few centuries out of her bag and sat it on a small table. For a moment, I had the sudden urge to smash it to pieces.

No. I couldn't do that. Shoving the desire down, I looked over at Aly. She was watching me with great interest.

"The couch is fine," I said, ignoring the question in her eyes. No need to get too personal, I'd be out of here before long.

"Alright," she drew out, seeming unconvinced by my answer. But then she moved further into the apartment. I followed after her, only half interested in where she lived.

Most of my masters had already been rich, or at least well off. Aly was neither of those things. The apartment was small and consisted of two rooms. The room held the couch she had mentioned, and a decent-sized bed. A small television sat near the couch with a beat-up coffee table in between them. A kitchen area, containing a two-person table, occupied the small space behind the couch. I could only assume the other room held the bathroom, which Aly entered and then exited moments later bearing a towel.

"Here," she handed it to me, "I only have a few towels, so just hang it on the bar when you are done taking a shower, so it dries out."

I tried to hold back the pity that welled up in me, but it was no use. How can someone live like this? I could walk across the whole apartment in a matter of seconds. Even my bedroom back home was bigger than this.

*Was.* I reminded myself.

I didn't have any of that now. In fact, I was worse off than my master. Nothing but a dusty old bottle to my name.

"Thanks," I said regretfully.

Aly shrugged a shoulder and moved over to the bed where she grabbed one of the pillows and took a blanket from the foot. She put the pillow on one end of the couch and spread the blanket out, giving me a particularly nice view of her backside.

As if she could feel my eyes on her, she straightened quickly and spun around. A blush covered her face, which I found endearing.

"So, you can sleep here, and I'm going to be over there." She pointed at her bed, avoiding my eyes.

"Alright," I moved over to the couch and sat down, testing out the cushions. The couch itself might not have looked like much, but at least it was comfortable.

Aly stood above me, her arms wrapped around her midsection. "Do you need anything else?"

"Are you going to make your wishes?" I couldn't help but ask.

Scowling, she dropped her arms and stomped toward the other room. When she slammed the door shut behind her, I sighed. This was taking forever.

I pulled my black boots off and, after a moment's thought, my t-shirt as well. If I was going to try and seduce her into making her wishes, I might as well start now. I stretched out on the couch not covering up with the blanket she had provided.

Aly reappeared again after a few moments, her work clothing swapped out for a t-shirt and a tiny pair of shorts that left her legs long and bare. Instead of her drooling over me, it was me who jumped up from my lounging position to watch her float across the room.

Her eyes did flicker my way briefly, but if she was affected by my muscled body, she wasn't giving anything away. I, on the other hand, couldn't keep my eyes off her form as she slipped into bed. Even in the poor lighting of the room, I could tell she had taken her undergarments off. The tips of her nipples protruded through her shirt, and I licked my lips.

"Goodnight," Aly's said in that sweet voice. Then she reached over next to her bed and pulled the switch on her lamp, putting us into darkness.

"Night," I answered laying back down on the couch. I lay there for a few minutes, but sleep eluded me. It wasn't until an annoying repetitive sound woke me that I even realized I had fallen asleep.

Groaning came from the bed, and I cracked my eyes open to see Aly's dark form turn over in the bed. A loud smack stopped the blaring noise, and then the light from her lamp blinded me.

Closing my eyes quickly, I turned my face away. More groaning from Aly and then there was a thud. The string of curses which came from my master's mouth caused me to open my eyes once more. She gripped her foot and glared down at the stack of books which I could only assume was the cause of her pain.

"Fuck," she muttered once more before she stomped across the room to dig through a pile of clothing in the corner. I watched with increasing interest as she discarded her shirt and shimmied out of her shorts. The tiny pink panties that covered her backside made me sit up on the couch.

The couch wasn't quiet, and the noise caused Aly to spin around. My eyes almost popped out of their sockets when they landed on her perfectly formed breasts. Each glorious globe was tipped with a rosy nipple that I ached to have in my mouth.

"What the hell?" Aly grabbed the nearest shirt to her and covered her chest. "You could have said something."

I shrugged and smirked at her. "If I had done that then you would have stopped."

"Of course, I would have." She picked up a shoe from the floor and chucked it at me. I ducked just in time, but it skimmed my shoulder causing a slight burn.

Rubbing my shoulder, my eyes following after her as she marched past me and into the bathroom. The door slammed behind her. I winced. *Well, that went well.*

I stood from the couch. Face scrunching up in pain, I stretched my muscles. The couch might seem comfortable, but it was killer on the back.

Not bothering to put my shirt on, I moved around the room. The only way I could describe Aly's apartment would be organized chaos. There were piles of clothes on either side of the room, one I assumed were for dirty ones and the other for clean. The books she had tripped over were only a few of a large stack next to a computer that'd seen better days.

I frowned. The last computer I'd seen had had a thicker screen and not as nice of a casing. The world had come further in technology than I'd thought.

The shower turned on in the bathroom just then, and I had the wicked idea to join my master. Closing my eyes, I envisioned her lovely breasts once more. My hands ached to touch them, to cup them in my palms and hear her squeal beneath me.

Shaking my head, I adjusted myself in my pants—which had become considerably tighter.

If I went in there, she'd just get mad again. Maybe even throw something else at me.

No. Aly seemed like the kind who needed a subtle seduction. Now, if it had been her friend Jade . . . I could have jumped into bed with her last night, and it would have been all over with by now.

The water turned off, and I leaned against the wall as I waited for her to come out. I didn't have to wait long. To my disappointment, Aly didn't come out in a towel but in a tank top and a pair of jeans that hugged her hips. Her wet hair brushed against her breasts which pushed up against the neckline displayed as if on a silver platter. Just for me. While a tiny towel would have been better, I was beginning to think I'd be attracted to her even if she wore a burlap sack.

"What are you looking at?" she snapped, all of last night's pleasantries gone.

"Just savoring the image." I smirked as she glared at me.

She went into the kitchen area and rummaged through the cabinets. Reaching up, she tried to grab something out of the cabinet but didn't seem to be able to reach it. With little more than a thought, I was suddenly behind her.

Aly jumped in place, my front firmly pressed against her back. I raised my hand and grabbed what she had been trying to reach. A box of some kind of breakfast bars. I shook my head, disgusted at the things these humans put in their bodies.

"Here you are." I held the box out to her and inhaled deeply. Her shampoo's scent was something floral and intoxicating. Much different than the sweet smell of her in the shop yesterday. Against my better judgment, I hardened against her, causing her to let out a gasp.

"Thanks," she murmured but didn't move from her position between me and the counter. I placed my hands on her hips and dipped my head until my nose brushed against her neck.

"You have the most tantalizing smell."

Her body stiffened, and then a shudder went through her. I was about to take things another step forward by pressing my mouth to her skin, but she moved abruptly out from my grasp.

"I've got to get to work," Aly said, her back to me as she began packing her bag. "I've got to open the shop for the morning shift and then go to class. I won't be done until this afternoon."

"Alright. I'll come with you." I followed after her, but she spun around and held a hand up, stopping me in my tracks.

"No," she snapped, but then changed her tone, "I mean, no. You should just stay here. I can't have you waiting for me in class. The teacher will have a fit." Aly's eyes move around the room looking at anything but at me.

"What do you expect me to do here?" I gestured to the disaster that was her home.

"You can watch T.V. or read a book," she suggested as she grabbed her keys and the other bag she had been carrying the night before. "Look, just stay out of trouble. You can leave the apartment if you want, but make sure you lock the door." Aly opened a drawer next to the door and handed me a metal key.

I frowned down at it, but before I could protest any further, she was out the door, leaving me alone.

Running a hand through my hair, I scanned the room. What the hell was I supposed to do now?

# CHAPTER 7
## *Alysha*

IT HAD TO HAVE been my worst performing day of my entire life. After leaving the apartment with my ever-tempting genie in my wake, I headed to the coffee shop.

Coffee and Stuff, thankfully, had remained exactly as it'd been the night before when I had locked up. Still dark out, I'd quickly unlocked the gate, opened the doors and did all the necessary opening jobs before Terry, the day-shift manager, came in.

Terry was gayer than the pride parade. With long stick-on lashes, and a face full of makeup, he made Tyra Banks look like a drag queen. And that was while wearing our god-awful uniform.

I was actually surprised Bruce ever hired him. My boss had, on more than one occasion, given the impression he was not as open-minded as the rest of us.

*But he got what was coming to him,* a small voice said in my head, and I batted it away. Bruce might be one of the least likely human beings I would save in a fire, but that didn't mean I should be speaking—or thinking—ill of him. Especially, when his predicament was my fault.

"Hey, sugar," Terry greeted me with a curious look, "I didn't know you were on today."

"I'm not," I answered before rounding the counter, "I'm just getting the shop open for you and then I'm off to class."

Terry's perfectly arched brows furrowed. "Where's boss man at?"

"Broken leg," I said, trying to sound nonchalant and not guilty. "He'll be out for a few days."

"Why're you doing his bidding? Isn't that what his assistant manager is for?" Terry asked me with a you-shoulda-known-better look.

Good question. The assistant manager, Lisa, also happened to be Bruce's on-again-off-again girlfriend. There was a betting pool on how long it would take before either Lisa quit or Bruce fired her. Their relationship was not the healthiest, to say the least.

"I don't know. I'm just doing what I'm told." I handed over the keys to Terry and headed for the door. "Don't break too many hearts today." I winked at him and he shooed me away, grinning.

It wasn't until I got down the block that I realized I'd forgotten to make the muffins for that day's business. I'd been so busy yesterday working a double, acting as manager, and dealing with Mac that I'd been too exhausted to even think about it.

I almost went back to tell Terry I'd make some quickly, but then shook my head. No. Class was more important. I couldn't miss any more days, or I'd flunk out. And that was the last thing I needed. Bruce would just have to deal with it, and if not, I had a spanking new genie I could use to change his mind.

A light bulb went off in my head. I had a genie who could grant me any wish I wanted! He could help me get a better job, hell he could get me the loan I needed to start my own shop. But as soon as the thought came I squashed it.

I wasn't in the habit of taking handouts and as far as I was concerned using a genie to make my life easier was just as bad. Nothing was worth having something you didn't work for yourself.

Sucking in a deep breath, I pushed my shoulders back and made myself finish the short trek to school.

Alinity wasn't a big town. The fact that it even had a community college was saying something. Out of the ten thousand people who lived in Alinity, at least three-fourths of them have gone to Alinity Community College at one point or another. Either for a degree, cooking classes, or just a sporting event.

I arrived just as the professor was getting ready to start class. I gave him an apologetic smile and made my way to my seat. I heard the professor greet the class, but then it seemed like it all blurred together after that.

My mind drifted to my unexpected guest. Last night, when I'd come out of the bathroom, it'd taken all my willpower to keep from ogling his shirtless form. If I thought he'd had muscles before, the sight of him bare-chested was enough to make even a nun need a change of underwear. I mean, lickable let-me-ride-you-like-a-surfboard kind of ripped. Just thinking of it now made my face heat up and I shifted in my seat.

What had been even worse was this morning.

Normally, I wasn't a morning person. There was a good reason I worked at a coffee shop. Well, besides the need for money. The unlimited supply of coffee was one of the only things that kept me going back. Even if it was on the pretty crappy side.

So, it was safe to say I wasn't completely aware of my surroundings when I first woke up. Which was why I really should clean up my apartment more. Tripping over books and other random items seemed like a daily habit for me. I'd only been doing what I usually did each morning before I'd remembered—well more like realized with a shock—that I still had a stranger in my home. But the way he had looked at me had almost been enough to make up for the fact that I'd just undressed in front of the genie.

The scorching longing in his eyes melted me all the way down to my very exposed panties. I'd darted out of the room more for my sanity than for modesty's sake.

My shower had been a cold one that still hadn't cooled my skin from the fire Mac had started in me. It had gotten even worse when he had taken the opportunity to press against me in the kitchen. Now *that* had been a happy experience.

What girl didn't want to know they were desired? Or have a to-the-nth-degree hottie pressing his hardened cock against them? Well, maybe not all of them. But I hadn't had any company of the male persuasion since the asshole-who-shall-not-be-named. And let's face it my battery-operated companion was just not the same.

Before I knew it, class was over, and I couldn't remember anything the professor had said. The rest of the day was pretty much the same. Too tired, and too distracted, to pay much attention or even take notes. I thought, not for the first time, that I should have just stayed home.

Finally, when my final class of the day had concluded, I was ready to climb back in bed and sleep for a week. But then I remembered my new roommate was waiting for me.

Hhmm. What to do about him? I couldn't keep him indefinitely, no matter how much I'd threatened I would. Mac had said the only way to get rid of him was to make my other two wishes.

Problem was, I had no idea what to wish for.

World peace? A Big Mac and fries? Just the thought of trying to keep a straight face while I told stuck-up-and-sexified-Mac I wanted to use one of my wishes for something I could buy myself made me smile. If he already had a bad opinion of humans, I doubted that kind of wish would help any.

Luckily, or rather unluckily considering the circumstances, I didn't have to worry about making my wishes. Sitting in the stairway in front of my door, was none other than asshole-who-shall-not-be-named.

"What are you doing here, Jared?" I asked, already ready to get it over with. We hadn't parted on good terms, or any kind of terms, to be honest. He'd up and left without a word, and with most of the contents of my bank account. To say I wasn't happy to see him was an understatement.

"Alysha." Jared scrambled up from the floor. He brushed his fingers through his short brown hair and adjusted his worn-out leather jacket. If there was one thing Jared loved more than anything, it was his jacket. He never went anywhere without it. Probably loved it more than he had ever loved me.

"I'm not in the mood to deal with you. Say your piece and then leave." I crossed my arms over my chest and tapped my foot in a rampant rhythm.

Jared frowned. Apparently, he had been under the impression I would be happy to see him. Boy, was he in for a rude awakening.

"Aren't you even a little bit happy to see me?"

See? A complete idiot.

"Why would you think that?" I snapped, not even bothering to pretend to be nice. "Unless you are here to apologize, or maybe even give me back all the money you stole from me, I don't have anything to say to you."

I tried to push by him to my door but he grabbed my arm. I glared down at his hand. "Let me go!"

"Not until you listen to me." Jared tightened his grip on my arm and jerked me so suddenly that I fell against him.

Before I could even try to get away from him, I was out of his arms and against an even more muscular chest. I glanced up to see Mac his eyes hard, and his kissable lips pressed so tightly together they were almost invisible.

"Is there a problem here?" Mac asked, though his tone made his words more of a warning than a question.

"Hey, back off man." Jared stepped toward us, puffing his chest out as he tried to intimidate Mac. "My girlfriend and I are just having a disagreement is all."

"Girlfriend?" Mac looked down at me an unhappy expression on his face.

"Ex-girlfriend," I corrected him. I moved a bit away from Mac so I could think of something other than how good he smelled and how much I wanted to rub myself up and down his form.

"Not for long," Jared had the gall to say. I shot him a scathing look before directing my attention back to Mac.

"Jared was just leaving. Don't worry about him."

"I'm not going anywhere until you talk to me." Jared shoved a finger at Mac and said, "You just go on your way buddy, and we won't have no problem."

I couldn't believe I ever dated this guy.

Mac's jaw tightened and he closed the distance between us once more. Placing his hand on my shoulder, he pulled me back to lean against him in an obvious statement to Jared he wasn't going anywhere.

"So this your new guy? You slutting it around with him now?" Jared focused his anger on me, "Bet you think you are some kind of shit now, with a guy like this."

"Yes, she is," Mac stated plainly, and I didn't try to correct him, "So, I'd be happy if you left my girlfriend and me alone now." The way he said it left no room for argument, but that had never stopped Jared before.

"Fine. I see how it is." Jared took a few steps back before giving me one last look. "This isn't over. We are going to talk. Soon."

When I heard the front door close behind him, I let out a heavy breath. Moving out of Mac's grasp, I gave him a small smile.

"Sorry about that. Thanks for helping out."

"You dated that man?" Mac asked, his expression not softening after Jared's departure.

"Unfortunately."

"He's not worthy of someone like you." He brushed my hair behind my ear his eyes searching my face. "Someone with your beauty should be adored and lavished with attention in public and in the bedroom."

I gave a nervous laugh, and Mac's heated gaze landed on me. Suddenly the stairway was ten times hotter, and my panties were soaked. Clearing my throat, I attempted to change the subject.

"Forget about him." I made a show of pushing Jared's visit behind me. Mac frowned but then gave me a curt nod. Glad he wasn't going to push the issue, I said, "I don't know about you, but I'm starving."

# CHAPTER 8
## *Mac*


AFTER THE INCIDENT BACK at Aly's home, I walked beside her in silence as she headed out to look for a place to eat. If Aly noticed my lack of conversation, she didn't say so. Instead, she kept prattling on about what had happened that day.

Not that I minded.

It was nice to have someone to talk to. My other masters weren't talkative types. At least not with me. I had spent the majority of my time alone. Or in my bottle. Hearing Aly talk about her day was a refreshing delight.

"This is my favorite place in the whole town. I'm sure you will just love it," Aly exclaimed animatedly as we came up on a building.

The building, painted deep red with large windows, didn't seem that impressive. Even more so the large triangle which sat on the top of a sign reading, "Leo's Pizzeria."

"You have had pizza before, right?" Aly quirked a brow at me, an inquisitive interest on her face.

"Pizza?" I pondered the word for a moment. I'd heard of it, but whether or not I had actually partaken of such a food, I couldn't recall.

"Yea!" Aly did a little jump in place. "It's the most delicious food group in the world and Leo makes the best in the state!"

I nodded in agreement though I didn't know who this Leo was or how a food could be a group of its own.

Aly led us through the glass doors and into the restaurant. The inside wasn't any more impressive than the outside. Obviously meant to be a family establishment, large tables filled most of the floor space while a few small booths sat along the walls. Black, white, and red decorated the place, the seats shining in a plastic-like covering. I forced myself not to curl my nose up in disgust. Aly liked this place, which meant I had to like it too.

My master led us up to the counter where a tall broad-shouldered man yelled into a window leading to the kitchen. He had dark hair which was cut long on top and tight on the sides. His goatee didn't do much to cover up his large guppy-like lips or the scar that covered one side of his face. The name tag on his button-up shirt said, "Leo." And I could only assume this was the man Aly had been talking about.

When Leo stopped yelling at his cook, he turned to the counter, mouth twisted in a scowl which was immediately replaced by a delighted grin at the sight of Aly.

I took a step closer to her, placing a hand on her shoulder. She looked up at me in question but didn't move away. Leo noticed my movement, and his grin faded for a moment before he forced it back into place.

"Hey, Aly," he greeted my master, his eyes never going to me, "I haven't seen you around for a while. What have you been up to?"

Aly smiled at him in a way that made my jaw clench. "Oh, you know, school keeps me pretty busy, and when I'm not there, Bruce has me working like a dog."

"I heard he broke his leg. That true?" Leo's gaze briefly brushed me before he turned his attention back to Aly.

My master's back stiffened under my hand at the mention of her boss's accident. A sudden wave of guilt came over me for my part in it. I pushed the feeling away and gave her shoulder a little squeeze.

Her dark eyes glanced up at me, and her lips lifted up slightly before she answered Leo's question. "Yeah, he tripped over a ladder. He's going to be out a few days. Which just means more work for me, sadly."

Leo shook his head, clear displeasure on his face. "You let that guy run you ragged. One of these days it'll be *you* in the hospital. You need to take better care of yourself."

"That's what I keep telling her," I jumped in, causing Aly and Leo to shoot me a surprised expression.

"Who's this guy? Your new guy?" Leo gestured to me with one hand, his face too guarded for me to tell if he approved or not.

Strangely enough, a part of me was anxious about Aly's answer. Why did I care if she told this guy I was her boyfriend or not? I didn't have any stake in her. I was only getting close to her to try and get her to make her wishes. She was my master, I, her genie. Nothing more.

"Mac is just a friend." Aly offered Leo a smile and pushed my hand off her shoulder. "Can we get a booth? I'm starving."

Seemingly satisfied with her answer, Leo grabbed two menus and led us over to a booth next to a family of five. Two adults and three toddlers to be exact. Dinner was not going to be quiet.

"Thanks, Leo." Aly took her seat and menu with a smile. "Can I get a coke and..." Her eyes moved to me in question.

I glanced down at the menu. Thankfully, the human language was similar enough to my own that I was able to find the drink options. Everything was sugary and carbonated. My stomach twisted at the thought of drinking such a concoction.

"I'll just have water," I answered finally, looking up to meet Leo's waiting gaze.

Leo wrote something on the little pad of paper he'd pulled out of his pocket. "Did you want your usual?" This question was directed at Aly, who chewed on her bottom lip before glancing up to me.

Not wanting to try and figure out the menu myself and hoping to get some points in, I said, "I trust your judgment."

Aly visibly relaxed and handed Leo her menu. "The usual is fine then, but make it a large this time."

Leo took both of our menus and gave a mock salute. "You got it, doll."

Once Leo went back to the counter, I asked, "So, what is your usual?"

"I thought you trusted me?" she teased, playing with the fork in front of her.

I smirked. "I do to a certain extent, and you are my master after all. If you weren't trustworthy, I wouldn't have been able to come to you."

She paused mid-spin of her fork and asked, "Is that how it works? You have to be worthy to have a genie? But what about all those other masters you had who took advantage of you?"

I shrugged. "Even the most trustworthy can turn. Having power changes people, and most of them for the worst."

"I'm not like that."

I watched her face as she said it. The rock-solid determination in her face almost had me thinking she might be telling the truth. But I'd been burned enough times to know humans. They might have good intentions, but they often led to the misfortune of others. And sometimes even themselves.

"I'm sure you aren't," I said carefully, and then tried to change the subject, "So, you are quite the popular woman." I nodded to Leo who couldn't stop looking over at our table.

Aly's eyes followed mine and then she shrugged as if it was nothing. "Leo's a good friend, but we've never dated . . . if that's what you mean. I was with Jared since high school, and after that, I wasn't interested in getting with anyone else."

"He hurt you badly, didn't he?" It wasn't really a question. I'd seen the way she had looked at him. It was the same way I had looked at my father when he had betrayed me to this existence. Though I was finally able to realize it hadn't been a betrayal, but a lesson. I highly doubted this Jared had the same intentions.

"I don't want to talk about it." Her voice was small as she stared hard at the table.

I opened my mouth to try to push the subject, but just then Leo returned with our drinks and a round wooden platter. Steam rose from the top, and the smell of it filled my nose. My stomach rumbled in response.

"Thanks, Leo." Aly shot the big man a blinding smile. She had meant it as a friendly gesture, but by the besotted look on the man's face, I could tell he had taken it as more.

Not bothering to point out Leo's admiration, I glanced down at the food before us. A bread-like substance covered the platter. The center of the bread held a dark red sauce layered with cheese, meat, and some yellow fruit.

I eyed it reluctantly and Aly laughed. The sound of it went straight to my groin. By the gods, she had a great laugh.

"What?" I asked, trying to make my voice sound irritated, but my desire for her overpowered it.

Still laughing, she pulled a piece of the pizza from the platter. "The look on your face . . . it's almost like you expect it to you jump out at you."

"I'm not scared of this food." I waved a hand at it. "In fact, I'm sure it is delightful." Cautiously, I slid my hand underneath the edge of the pizza as

Aly had done, and pulled a piece of it off. Picking it up, my mouth watered even as I took a large bite of it. Which was a mistake. My hand shot up to my mouth at the sudden heat, and I tried to fan my tongue off while trying not to spit the bite out.

"Sorry, I should have told you it was hot." Aly frowned and handed me a napkin. I snatched it from her hand gratefully and spat the piece into it.

"Hot?" I cried out in disbelief. "More like molten lava."

Aly rolled her eyes. "Stop being such a baby. It's not that bad." To prove her point, she took a bite of her own pizza and easily swallowed it. "See."

"Mine must be defective." I glared down at the food on my plate. "Let me try yours." I leaned over the table and before she could protest, took a bite of the cheese monstrosity in her hand.

"Hey!" She pulled the pizza out of my reach so I couldn't take another bite.

I sat back in my seat and grinned. "Yours is far superior to the slice I had. The Leo man must have done it on purpose."

"Oh, yeah right." She rolled her eyes again. "Because he cares so much about burning your mouth he kept your half in the oven longer."

"He cares for you," I pointed out with a raised brow, "And why shouldn't he? You are a hard worker."

"Ha."

"A great baker."

"You've never even eaten my food." Her lips pressed together in doubt, but the edges fought not to smile.

I placed my elbows on the edge of the table and leaned forward as I murmured, "And a fantastic pair of tits."

"Mac!" she cried out, her eyes darting around the room as a blush covered her face.

I shrugged. "It's true."

"Still, we are in a public place. With children for god's sake." She gestured wildly around her, but the smile on her face showed me she wasn't as upset as her words indicated. "Besides, you weren't supposed to see them anyways."

"Shouldn't have or not, they are still the highlight of my millennia and is very nearly putting you at the top of my list of favorite masters."

"Really?" Her eyes widened and I couldn't help but grin.

"Most definitely." I gave a short nod as I took a cautious bite of my pizza, which had now cooled to an acceptable temperature.

"So, what would make me hit the top of that list?" The eagerness in her voice made me harden painfully. My mind imagined hearing that eagerness as she asked me for something else entirely. Something best not thought about around children.

Adjusting myself beneath the table, I picked up my water and mock saluted her. "You'll just have to wait and see."

# CHAPTER 9

## *Alysha*

DURING THE REST OF meal, my face felt like it was on fire, and I couldn't stop smiling. Somehow this guy, this genie had found a direct line to my libido and, strangely enough, my heart.

At first, I had thought Mac was an egotistical asshole. I had had every intention of keeping him at arm's length and out of my way. Problem was, to get rid of him completely meant making my wishes but the more I got to know the mysterious genie the less important that seemed to be.

The tension between us on the way home was overpowering. When we arrived at my apartment, my nerves skyrocketed at the thought of being alone with him. Now that there wasn't a public place, or other people in the way, there was nothing to keep us from exploring the sexual energy between us.

"So," I started, placing my keys in their designated spot on the table by the door. I slowly twisted around to face Mac and leaned back against the small table. His eyes meet mine, and for a moment, I thought he was going to take that next step. The one that I longed to take but was too chicken to. But the moment was over before either of us did anything, and an awkwardness filled the space.

"I'm going to go take a shower," Mac said.

"Uh, okay," I replied and then gave him a half smile. "I'll be right here."

*Lame, Alysha. So lame.*

My gaze trailed after Mac as he moved across the room to pick up the towel I had given him the night before. I didn't even try to pretend I was interested in something else as he walked to the bathroom door and then shut it behind him without a backward glance.

My shoulders sagged, and I let out a heavy breath. "Fucking Christ," I growled at myself. "What is the matter with you? You act like he's the first guy you've ever been in lust with!"

The door to the bathroom opened and Mac popped his head out, startling me. "Where are your bathing supplies?"

With a shaky hand, I pointed to the bathroom and said, "In a basket beneath the sink."

Mac glanced behind him and then turned back to me to say, "Thanks," before he closed the door once more.

I collapsed against the table. It wobbled, almost tipping me onto the ground. Quickly standing up, I searched around my apartment for something to keep myself busy and not think about the very naked, very wet genie in my bathroom.

I grabbed my book bag off the ground and pulled out my statistics book. Statistics had been one of today's classes in which I hadn't been paying attention. I was lucky the professor had outlined all the homework assignments in the syllabus at the beginning of the semester, or I would have been screwed.

Pulling the paper out, I scanned down until I found today's date and groaned. Ten pages to read and at least a dozen problems to get through.

Well, at least I wouldn't be thinking of Mac's rippling abs as the water trailed down and wrapped around his . . .

I shook my head, snapping out of my daydream. *No, don't go there, Aly.* I forced my attention back to the book in front of me and began to read that day's assignment.

The subject must have been boring because Mac's hand was my shoulder shaking me awake. I'd fallen asleep on the couch. I blinked up at him in confusion, and then my gaze dipped down, taking in his bare chest and the towel barely wrapped around his waist. If I just reached out, I could pull it off and see what was beneath it.

My hand itched to do just that, but Mac's voice stopped me from actually performing the action. Blinking once more, I yawned. "What?"

Mac smirked down at me with a knowing look. "I said, do you happen to have any other clothing I could wear. Or maybe you could wash these?" He held up the clothes he had previously been wearing.

"Can't you just magic yourself some new clothes?" I asked, frowning at the bundle in his hands while at the same time trying not to think about his almost nude form.

He sighed and tossed his clothes on the couch beside me. "I wish it were that simple. I might have the ability to grant your wishes, but I can't make things appear out of thin air for myself. So I have to rely on getting new clothes whenever I am out of my bottle."

"But you were able to disappear and reappear so easily. How is that any different?" I got up from the couch and moved past him, making sure I didn't touch his bare skin.

"That's different."

"How so?" I asked over my shoulder as I made my way to my pile of clean clothing. I knew I had something of Jared's in there somewhere. Of course, they were completely different sizes, but hopefully I could find something that would fit him. I made a mental note to take him to Wal-Mart later.

"We are bound by the bottle. My magic wants to be close to you, so all I have to do is let it," he explained, and then suddenly his slightly damp chest was right in front of my face.

"See?" He smiled down at me and I gulped.

Taking a step back, I handed him a shirt and pair of sweatpants. "Here, they won't fit perfect, but they'll do until I can get you some real clothes."

"Thanks." Mac took the clothes from my hands, and the electricity that went through the spot where our hands had touched ran a direct line to my nub.

"Uh, yeah. No problem," I muttered as my eyes kept locking onto the kissable lips just inches from mine. I took a step backward, and my foot caught on one of the many objects littering my floor.

I let out an alarmed cry, but instead of hitting the ground, a pair of warm arms wrapped around my waist. Pulled flush against the very chest I had been ogling, I became acutely aware of Mac's thoughts on our position. And he was happy. Very happy.

My eyes met Mac's as I breathed out, "Good catch."

"So, as you can see," his voice rumbled through his chest and into mine, shooting straight down my spine, "My body wants to be near you . . . almost desperately."

His words brushed against my mouth as his face lowered toward mine. My skin burned where his hands held me close, one on my back and another on my lower hip. I forced myself not to arch into his touch.

A brush of lips was all it took to open the floodgates. Mac's mouth engulfed mine as my hands came up to wrap around his neck. Our tongues tangled together, his taste an intoxicating mixture of the Hawaiian pizza we'd just had and his own flavor. I ran my tongue along his teeth, and he nipped at it causing a moan to slip from my lips.

Mac's hands dipped down to cup my backside. My legs automatically came up to wind around his waist, pushing myself closer to him. When our centers met, we groaned in unison and paused to take in the feeling. Then we were kissing again. Mac stumbled through the pile of stuff on the floor and then my back was pressed against the wall.

Even that wasn't enough for him because one minute I was kissing Mac in the middle of my tiny apartment and the next a weird rippling came over me. I pulled away from him and opened my eyes. Mac leaned over me and from the softness beneath my back and the familiar ceiling, I knew I was lying on my bed. I didn't have a chance to even question it before my genie took my mouth once more.

My legs spread apart on their own as Mac settled between them. The position more intense than the last, it didn't take long before it was only reasonable that we would either have to stop or go to the next level.

Mac moved away from me and reached down. I stopped his hand as it grabbed hold of the towel around his waist. He frowned at me, his eyes questioning.

"Wait," I said, my voice husky and breathless, "Too fast."

At my words, Mac dropped his hand and shifted off me. He sat beside me on the bed, and I moved slowly into a sitting position as well. We were silent for a few moments, neither one of us looking at the other.

Mac broke the silence first. "I'm sorry if I crossed a line. It's been a long time since I've been with anyone, let alone someone as tempting as you."

My face heated at his words and I ducked my head down to hide my grin. "It's alright. I haven't been with anyone in a while either."

"Not even Jared?"

I frowned at the mention of my ex. "No, we have been done for a long time, and there is no way I would ever get back with him. Even for a triple berry tart." I shot him a lopsided grin hoping to ease the tension.

He smiled back at me in return, and I relaxed a bit. Mac got up off the bed, and the towel slipped down. Licking my lips, I almost hoped it would fall, but then chastised myself for being such a pervert. I was the one who had wanted to slow down. I couldn't have it both ways.

"I guess I'd better get dressed," Mac winked and then scooped his clothes off the floor where he'd dropped them and made his way to the bathroom. I wasn't ashamed to admit I'd watched his butt the entire way there. When he closed the door behind him, I collapsed on the bed.

What a crazy two days. I'd gone from hating my job and wishing bodily harm upon my boss, to having my own genie who'd fulfilled that very wish and who now might end up being even more than just a stranger. So maybe the bodily harm part was pretty bad. I winced. Okay, a lot bad. But that was before we had started to get to know each other.

And now. I sighed and clasped my hands over my heart. Now, I was on the verge of jumping his genie bones.

I needed to be more careful. While a one-night stand was all good and well—Jade would even have applauded it—I couldn't do that with Mac. I still had two more wishes left, and then he would be gone. So if we started anything, it would be only temporary, and I had to make sure my heart knew that.

As I slipped under the covers, I frowned hard. The likelihood that I'd be able to separate myself enough to take advantage of what Mac was clearly offering was slim. I'd never been a love-'em-and-leave-'em type. Doubted I ever would be. Which meant unless I was prepared for heartbreak, I shouldn't let anything else happen between me and the delectable Mac.

Letting out an aggravated breath, I plopped back on my pillows. I'd just have to keep my distance from him. Make sure we weren't alone longer than needed.

Just then Mac came out of the bathroom wearing only the sweatpants. They were tight on him, as I'd thought they might be, and hung low on his hips showing a delicious line pointing straight to his . . .

Cold showers. I would need lots and lots of cold showers.

# CHAPTER 10
## *Mac*

WHEN I WOKE UP the next morning, Aly was already gone. Her alarm made the annoying buzzing noise, and it took me a good five minutes to figure out how to shut it off.

After I shut the damn contraption off, I started back to the couch but then looked at the larger, more comfortable option, which was now thankfully vacant. Glancing around the dim room, I searched out Aly's bag and noticed it was gone. The keys to the apartment were gone as well.

Must have gone to work. I shrugged, then wasted no time throwing myself into her bed. Which I immediately regretted.

It smelled like her. I rubbed my face against her pillow and inhaled deeply. Just her scent caused me to harden. I let out a frustrated growl. Why couldn't I stop thinking about her? She was just one human woman. I'd been with plenty of other women, more attractive women, and I never thought about them afterward. I hadn't even bedded Aly, and I couldn't get her off my mind.

But last night had been something. Kissing her was almost worth the time and effort I was taking in seducing her, although it didn't seem so much like a chore to just get her to make her wishes. Now, I was actually looking forward to having her beneath me once more. To hear those little sighs of pleasure fall from her lips.

From what she'd told me I assumed that Jared fellow had been her only lover. He didn't seem like he knew how to pleasure a woman. Or even care about anything but his own release. My lips quirked. *Oh, all the things I could teach her.*

It wasn't until the light from the window shone into my eyes that I realized I had fallen asleep. I groaned as I rolled over. It was far more comfortable than the couch and even harder to leave.

My stomach rumbled, reminding me that though I was a genie I still had to eat. I inched out of bed and was thankful Aly wasn't there to see me that way. As I flipped on the light, I noticed a pile of clothes on the kitchen counter.

I walked over to the pile and picked up the note sitting on top. 'I had to guess at your size, so hopefully these fit. I'll be off work at five.'

Smiling at the little heart she had placed next to her name, I sat the note aside. I picked up the first item, a dark blue t-shirt, and pulled it over my head. It was a bit looser than my normal clothing, but it would do. Next were the pants. Those fit like a glove, but not so much that I couldn't button them.

After slipping on the clothing Aly had left for me, I found my shoes. I glanced around the kitchen and contemplated hunting through her cabinets for something to eat. The prospect wasn't appealing. Yesterday I'd eaten some kind of cereal which had been more akin to cardboard than food. I didn't care to repeat it.

Then I remembered Aly worked at a coffee shop. They were bound to have some kind of breakfast food.

I searched the table next to the apartment door for the key Aly had given me. I locked the front door and made my way down the stairs. Once I was out on the street, I tried to remember where the coffee shop was located.

"Idiot," I muttered to myself. Only yesterday I had explained how the contract between Aly myself worked, and I had just forgotten it. I closed my eyes and let my magic search out Aly's presence. I found her a few miles away and promptly transported myself outside of the shop.

Aly's gaze shot to the window the moment I appeared. Eyes wide, her usual friendly grin faltered. As I opened the door, I heard her tell her customer to have a good day, and the woman turned from the counter not realizing I had just appeared out of thin air.

I walked up to the counter, offering her a scorching grin. She didn't return it. Instead she glared at me with her hands on her hips. Strangely, it only made her more attractive.

"What the hell do you think you're doing?" she whispered harshly, her eyes darting over to her friend Jade, who gave us a knowing grin.

"Coming to visit you at work of course." I leaned across the counter and tried to kiss her, but she moved away. I frowned. "What's wrong?"

"You can't just pop up wherever you like. Someone could have seen you!" Aly gestured at the customers, concern etched on her face.

"Oh," I said, then waved her off, "Don't worry about that. My magic has a condition that ensures those who aren't bound to me won't notice my arrival unless they are staring right at me. Even then most will just brush it off."

Aly growled. "You couldn't have told me this the first day? I was freaking out for nothing!"

I gave her an apologetic smile. "I wasn't planning on liking you then. I wasn't about to make it easier for you."

"You what?" Aly's mouth fell open, and I couldn't help but chuckle.

Chucking her under the chin with my knuckle, I repeated, "I like you, Aly. Quite a lot, actually. More than I should."

She ducked her head the way she did when she was embarrassed, then tucked a hair behind her ear. "I like you too, Mac."

"Great! We all like each other. Now, can I get my coffee?" I turned around to see a man in his mid-forties standing behind me. He scowled at me, but then swallowed down whatever he was about to say when I stood to my full height.

"I'm sorry," I crossed my arms over my chest, "Are we bothering you?"

The man shook his head, his mouth open wide, "No, no. It's fine, take your time."

"Thank you." I smirked and clapped him on his shoulder. I tried to resume my mission to seduce Aly, but she angled her neck to look around me.

"Sorry, sir. I'll be right with you," she said to the man. Then to me, she said, "If you are going to stay, you have to sit over there." She pointed at the table I'd sat at the first day.

Giving her a bored look, I shifted away from the counter and sat at the table. Crossing my ankles, I leaned back in my seat to watch Aly work. I hadn't been sitting there long when her friend, Jade, came by.

*Great. Here we go again.*

I didn't have anything against the woman, but the way she had thrown herself at me the first day had been off-putting. Even more so when she'd later talked about her beau.

Her multi-toned hair was pulled up in a high ponytail that bounced as she walked. She slid into the chair on the opposite side of the table. Pushing a cup of light-colored liquid and one of the mouthwatering muffins in front of me, she smiled.

"Thought you might be hungry waiting over here," she explained as I devoured the muffin. My eyes closed briefly as the confection filled my mouth. It was exquisite. It took everything I had not to let out a moan of pleasure. And with Jade's amused gaze on me, I didn't dare.

"Good, aren't they?" Jade nodded to the muffin with a proud grin.

"They're the best thing I've ever tasted," I replied honestly.

"Aly makes them."

My eyes widened at the news. My eyes locked onto Aly who was busy helping another customer. Not only was she a hard worker but she could bake as well? Was there anything she couldn't do?

"Why is she working here then?" I turned slightly in my chair to ask Jade. "She could have her own shop selling these masterpieces!"

Jade shrugged a sad shoulder. "I know, and she does too, but her last guy really screwed her over."

"You mean Jared?" I asked, my lips pressing into a thin line.

"Oh, Aly told you about the jerkwad, did she?" Her brows lifted in surprise.

"He came by the apartment while Aly was at class," I explained, my gaze straying back over to my master.

"What were you doing at Aly's apartment?" Jade asked, amusement in her eyes. Then she shook her head. "Never mind, I don't need to know. Aly's a big girl. What happened with the ex?"

Finishing off the final piece of the muffin, I searched out the ones sitting on the counter, staring longingly at them. Before I could ask Jade jumped up and fetched another one, then handed it to me with a laugh.

"Here. Aly hasn't had a guy in a while. She forgets that you need to be fed." Jade leaned forward, resting her cheek on her hand.

Frowning at her, I took a bite of the muffin and said, "I'm not a pet."

Jade only laughed at my denial. "Sure, you aren't. So anyways, dish. What happened?"

Swallowing the piece in my mouth, I asked, "Why don't you just ask Aly? She was there too."

The humor in her face dropped, and she sneaked a look at her friend, "Aly might act like what happened with Jared doesn't bother her, but it does. She doesn't like to talk about him. I doubt she would tell me even if I asked."

"But aren't you her best friend?"

Jade shrugged, "There are some things that even best friends shouldn't know about. She doesn't want to talk about it, so I don't push. She'll open up when she's ready."

We fell into a comfortable silence for a few moments before Jade spoke up again, "Well, no matter what happened, I'm glad she has you. I haven't seen her this happy in a while. Whatever you are doing, keep up the good work."

She stood from the table and winked before heading back behind the counter to help Aly, who gave her a questioning look before her eyes met mine across the room. I waved and offered her a small smile. Her face flushed and she ducked her head down before greeting the next customer.

There certainly was more to my new master than met the eye. The ex-boyfriend who—from Jade's explanation—she didn't talk about, her ability to put up with her less-than-appealing boss and go to school at the same time, not to mention her wonderful muffins. If I ever got back home, I'd have to commission her to make some for me to share with the others. There certainly wasn't anything like it there.

Thinking about home made my chest tighten. If Aly completed her other two wishes, I might never see her again. And if she was the last one I needed to break the spell then I, for sure, would go home and the likelihood of ever seeing her again would be even smaller.

I took a sip of the cup of what I could only assume was coffee, and grimaced. Even with the added sweetness, the drink was barely palatable. I glanced up and down the line of customers and wondered how they could stand it. Then I noticed each one of them was purchasing one of Aly's muffins with their drink.

Anger filled me. Obviously, the only reason her boss kept her around was to counter his disgusting product. If it hadn't been for her muffins, I doubt the shop would even still be running. It made me wonder even more why she let him treat her so badly, and why she didn't just branch out on her own.

Then, what Jade had said came back to me. Was this Jared guy really the source of all her problems? If so, maybe Jade was right. If she wouldn't talk to her best friend maybe, just maybe, I could get her to talk to me. Then I could get her to use one of her wishes to fix it.

# CHAPTER 11
## *Alysha*

MAC SAT AT THE table I had sent him to. He remained there through both the breakfast rush and then through the lunch rush. I felt bad. I'd been so focused on making sure I kept things up and running at the store that I hadn't even thought of taking him something to eat.

Thankfully, Jade had helped me out on that front. So, when the lunch rush finally died down, I decided it was my turn to take care of my genie.

"Hey," I said as I came around the counter to stop in front of Mac. The clothes I had bought him weren't perfect by any means, but they didn't detract from his general deliciousness.

Mac stood from the table, and I was once again reminded of his towering height. It didn't intimidate me the way it might some other women. Instead, it made me feel safe. As if he could really take care of himself and of me.

"Sorry, I kind of forgot about you over here." I tried to make my voice reveal how sorry I was, but I was too tired, and I ended up sounding more strained than apologetic.

"You've been busy." Mac's eyes crinkled on the sides as he smiled down at me.

"Yeah, you'd think these people would learn by now that the coffee sucks around here." I gave a nervous laugh and pushed my hair behind my ear.

"It's not the coffee they come for." An unreadable expression crossed his face. One that made my cheeks heat up.

"You liked my muffins, huh?" I glanced at the crumbs scattered on his table.

Stepping closer to me, he took me by the hips and murmured, "There's only one other thing I could imagine tastes better than those delicious creations."

I made a choking sound and scanned the shop, worried someone would hear the double meaning in his words. But no one was paying us any mind. Well, besides Jade, who wasn't even trying to pretend she wasn't eavesdropping.

"Um, why don't we run down to the sandwich shop and get us some lunch, okay?" I pressed a palm against his chest, and he dropped his hands.

Waving at Jade, I walked out of the store and turned right. I didn't need to look behind me to know Mac had followed. The heat from his body warmed my skin, and something inside of me urged me closer. I slowed down slightly, so we were walking side by side.

"Your friend Jade really cares about you," Mac said after a moment.

"Yeah, she's great."

"She wanted to know about what happened with your ex-boyfriend yesterday."

I stopped in my tracks and then started back up again. "She did?" I asked cautiously. As my best friend, I usually told Jade everything. Except when it came to Jared.

When Jared and I had originally started dating, we'd been great together. Everyone had been so happy for us that it had almost been like a dream. Even Jade hadn't been able to find fault in him, and she could find an error in a twenty-foot painting. Believe me, she did it once!

Then suddenly, Jared started investing. Which turned into him needing to borrow money. At first, it was only a little bit here and there. Then it became large amounts and cosigning loans and credit cards. I'd been young and in love. I hadn't known any better.

Eventually, I'd realized what was happening and had told him no more. He'd argued with me and had even grabbed me once. Hard enough to leave bruises. That had been it for me.

I'd never told Jade how bad it had actually gotten. Or how much worse it could have been if I hadn't gotten out. And I still didn't plan on telling her, or anyone else either.

"She's worried about you," Mac said after a moment when I didn't follow up my question with an explanation.

"I'm sure she is," I replied and then snuck a look at his face. His brows were furrowed, and a frown marred his lips. I sighed. "Don't worry about it. He won't bother us anymore."

"But what if he does?"

"Then I'll deal with it," I snapped and then sighed again. "I know what you are going to say."

"Really?" Mac smirked. "What am I going to say?"

I crossed my arms over my chest and came to a stop. "That I should just use one of my wishes to get rid of him."

Mac tucked his hands into his pockets and rocked back on his heels as he asked, "Then, why don't you?"

I unfolded my arms and gestured wildly. "Because magic can't solve all my problems. That's something I have to just do on my own. I've done fine so far. Why give in now?"

"But what if I want to help you?" Mac took a step toward me, his fingers brushing my cheek. "What if I don't want to see you hurt?"

I brushed his hand away. "You can't do magic without me making a wish, remember? It's part of the rules."

"Right." Mac dropped his hand and stepped back.

"Anyways, we're here." I waved a hand at the building next to us. Mac turned around to look at the place.

The only sandwich shop in town was a mom-and-pop place called Walter's. Whether or not the original owner's name was Walter, I didn't know. The current owners were a cute little Middle Eastern couple who always gave me extra pickles.

I walked up to the counter and ordered my usual, which also happened to be Jade's, and then asked Mac what he wanted. He studied the menu for a long while before finally placing his order.

"Are you sure?" I asked after he gave the teenager at the register his order. "That has peppers and hot sauce on it."

Giving me a lopsided grin, he nodded. "I like hot food." I stared him down until he added, "Flavor-wise, not temperature."

We waited in silence as our orders were made. When our number was called, I reached for the bags, but Mac beat me to it with a grin. Instead, of arguing about feminism and all that, I let him carry them. After all, I'd been working all day, while he had just sat there.

We remained silent on the way back, but every time our hands brushed against each other a little shiver would run through me. I almost grabbed his hand just to get it over with, but he beat me to it. Except, instead of just holding my hand, he dragged me into a narrow alley between two buildings.

"What are you doing?" I asked before he pressed me against the brick wall and covered my mouth with his.

My arms wrapped around his neck automatically and I arched on my toes to get closer. The bags in his hands dropped to the ground, and I tried to pull away to check on them, but Mac cupped my breast, and my mind went blank. His mouth worked down from my lips to my neck where he found a particularly sensitive spot and bit down on it.

I let out a delighted squeal which turned into a throaty moan as his hands worked their magic on my chest. When I started rubbing myself against him like a cat in heat, I realized we had to stop before it went any further.

"Wait," I said, pushing him back a little bit, "I thought we were going to slow down?"

"This isn't slow?" He smirked and looked me over. "You have more clothes on now than last night."

He had me there. But while every fiber of my being screamed at me to say screw it and let him have his way with me, we *were* in a public place. And I didn't feel like getting arrested.

I didn't answer his question. Instead, I bent down and picked up the bag he had dropped. Luckily, it hadn't torn open, and all of our food was still sitting nicely inside. Shooting Mac a chastising glare—which I didn't really mean—I started down the sidewalk once more.

We arrived back at the shop just in time. Jade was getting swamped, and I handed the bag quickly over to Mac so I could help her. When we were done clearing out the line, Jade and I sat down at the table with Mac.

"We'd better eat quickly," Jade commented. "They are like ravaging raptors today."

Mac gave me a questioning look, and I leaned over to whisper to him, "It's a dinosaur. You know a large lizard-like creature."

With a nod, Mac turned back to his food. I didn't know if he understood what I was talking about. If he didn't know what a dinosaur was, then they must not have existed in his world. Come to think of it, I didn't know much about him at all.

A customer came through the door, but before I could get up to help them, Jade jumped up and said, "I've got this."

With Jade away from the table, I took the moment to voice my curiosity.

"So, Mac," I said after a few bites into my sandwich, "What's your home like?"

The genie paused mid-bite and stared at me as if he'd never expected that I would ask about him. He took another bite of his sandwich, which he did, in fact, enjoy in spite of the hot ingredients. He chewed for a moment, swallowed and then said thoughtfully, "Different."

I wanted to pull my hair out. It was such a guy answer. As a genie, I would have expected him to give me something more than that. I knew if I was some magical being forced to keep a secret, I'd want to spill my guts the moment I could.

"Come now, you know all about me. And Jade's going to be back any minute. You have to give me something," I egged him on, trying to get just a tiny bit more insight into his world.

"Well, we don't have cars, for one."

I nodded. "I expected that. If you can all poof where you want, there really isn't a point to it, is there?"

"Oh, we can't all do that." Mac shook his head. "We walk most places, or ride a horse." He glanced up at the ceiling for a moment and tapped his chin. "Come to think of it though, it's not much bigger than your town here."

"What isn't?"

"Tavokia," Mac stated simply, taking another huge bite of his sandwich.

"Tavokia," I said slowly. "Is that where you live?"

"Uhuh, I'm the crown prince actually. Or well I was." His brow furrowed as he frowned.

"Wow," my brain swirled with the knowledge, "To think I've been housing a real prince. But what are you doing acting as a genie? Shouldn't you be taking care of your kingdom?"

Mac winced. "Well, about that. I got in trouble, you see," I motioned for him to go on, "You know the way I was when we first met?"

"You mean an arrogant asshole?" I asked with a smile.

He shot me a warning look, then continued, "Yeah, well, I used to be much worse. So bad that my father thought I needed to learn a lesson. And so, here I am," he held his arms out to the sides, "Stuck on your plane until whatever spell he put on me is satisfied I have learned humility. Then I can go home."

"Man," I said after a moment, "That sucks."

"You know what else sucks?" Jade called from the counter. "Working by myself."

My attention darted to the line that had grown quite a bit since Jade had gotten up. I sat the rest of my sandwich down and hurried to help her.

"Sorry about that," I said as I took her place behind the register.

"Don't worry about it." She waved my apology off. "If I was you, I wouldn't be able to pay attention to anything else but that man candy."

Laughing at her description, I twisted around to take the cup from her. The look on her face changed from teasing to worry as her eyes focused on something behind me.

"Uh oh," Jade said as the door to the shop opened up.

"What?" I asked, a grin still on my face. When my eyes followed hers to the door, my smile disappeared. Jared stood in the line, an eager expression on his face. "What the hell are you doing here?"

# CHAPTER 12

## *Mac*

THE MOMENT JARED WALKED into the shop, I jumped up from my seat. A determined expression set on his face as he made his way straight to the counter where Aly stood frozen to the spot.

I stepped forward to try and stop him, but Aly unfroze long enough to shake her head at me. I dropped my arm but didn't sit back down. Forced to remain on the sidelines while she took care of it, I waited for my chance to get the guy out of there.

Wished for or not, Jared wasn't going to stay around long.

Thankfully for Aly, the line had died down, or I had no doubt the scumbag would have just cut in front of everyone. The satisfied look on his face was enough to make me want to punch him. But I stayed away because it was what Aly wanted. Not as if she'd wished for it.

*As if that would stop you?* a voice in my head taunted.

Ignoring the voice, I tried to listen to what Aly and her ex were talking about. From the displeasure on her face, it couldn't be anything good.

"You can't just come in here. This is my job," Aly told Jared, pure venom in her voice.

If Jared could tell she was upset, he didn't show it. He placed his hands on the counter and leaned over the register, a desperate expression on his face.

"You won't talk to me at your home. What choice did I have?"

Aly crossed her arms over her chest and sniffed. "For good reason."

"Come on, Aly. Babe." Jared reached over the counter and tried to grab her arm, but she stepped out of his reach. "So, it's going to be like that? After everything we've been through you won't even let me touch you. Talk to you? You at least owe me that."

Even I knew the idiot's words were wrong. Aly's face reddened, and her fingers curled into fists. Excitement took hold of me as I hoped she would finally put him in his place.

Sadly, before Aly could so much as draw her arm back, Jade stepped in. She took hold of Aly's hand—which had begun to rise up from her side—and clasped it in her own.

Shooting Aly a warning look, Jade turned her fiery gaze on Jared. "She doesn't owe you anything."

"You mind your own business. Leech," Jared sneered at Jade, his eyes scanned up and down Jade's form in obvious disdain. I swore if Jade hadn't wanted to hit the man before, she was ready to hit him in Aly's place.

"You're one to talk," Jade argued, stepping up to the counter. They were beginning to draw the attention of the other customers, which Aly had noticed too. She pulled Jade back from the register and gave Jared an icy glare.

"I don't have anything to say to you. I don't owe you anything. You ruined any chance for that last time. Now, you need to go before I call the cops." Aly pointed a finger toward the door, a firm determination her face.

"But babe..." Jared tried to plead one more time.

"Go!" She shoved her finger at the door once more, and I started forward. If he wouldn't go on his own, I'd be happy to help him out.

Jared spun on his heels and when he saw me, stopped in his tracks. Scanning me up and down, his face said he clearly found me lacking. But whatever he thought he had that I didn't, I wasn't sure I wanted.

"Good luck with that one," Jared gestured with his head, "she's a right bitch."

"I think I'll take my chances," I replied, earning me a look of disgust as Jared marched out of the shop.

When he was gone, I turned back to the counter where Jade was talking quietly to Aly. My master's face was red, and her eyes glistened. She must have felt me watching because she glanced up and my chest constricted. The devastation on her face was almost too much to bear.

Before I could reach her, Aly took off to the back leaving me with Jade. Placing my hands on the counter, I strained my neck to see around the corner, hoping to see the woman who had so captivated me in such a short while. But it was no use.

"What an asshole," Jade commented, and I turned my attention to her.

"Yes, he is in fact," I agreed and then frowned, "But what I can't figure out is what happened between those two that makes his appearance so jarring."

A shadow covered Jade's face. "Like I said before, I don't know what all happened. She won't tell me. But I do know that he used her, financially, emotionally. You name it."

"Did he abuse her?" Anger stirred in my heart at the thought of that lowly filth laying a hand on such a sweet woman like Aly.

Jade shook her head. "Not that I know of. Doesn't mean he didn't though. Aly never said. What's worse though is he's the reason she is stuck in this place."

"What do you mean?"

Letting out a bitter laugh, Jade began restocking the counter. "You don't think she's at this shit job by choice, do you?"

"I thought she just needed the money until she finished school or something like that." Even as I said the words it didn't seem plausible. There were plenty of other jobs out there. She could have easily taken up one of those.

"Not the fuck likely," Jade scoffed. "She's stuck here cause that ass-wipe ruined her." Jade sighed at my puzzled frown. "This is a small town, Mac. People talk. Especially when it involves money."

"Okay?" I drew out.

"Aly is a great girl. An amazing baker, but she's too trusting. Too naive for her own good. She really got bit in the ass when it came to Jared. He kept borrowing money from her, promising he'd pay it back. He'd have her co-sign on loans for startup companies that were sure to make them millions but . . ." Jade let out a heavy breath and shook her head, "they all turned out to be crap. Leaving Aly to pay the bills and no money, or credit, of her own to realize her dream."

"Which is?" I quirked a brow at the blue-haired woman.

"To start her own bakery of course." Jade tossed a few plastic sticks at me. "For her new boyfriend, you sure are slow."

"Boyfriend?"

This time it was Jade's turn to raise a brow. "Oh, are you guys not labeling it yet? Would 'lovers' be a more accurate description?"

My lips moved up at the edges at her words. "I haven't had the pleasure."

"Seriously?" The disbelief in her voice was pronounced. "She's had you in her apartment, and you two haven't even done the nasty yet?" When I shook my head, she scowled. "Has that girl learned nothing from me? I swear it's like talking to a wall."

"Well, it's not for the lack of trying, but I believe Aly would say we are getting to know each other first." I held my hands out in defense.

"Ha. That sounds like her." Jade clicked her tongue. "Well, she has better self-control than me. If I had my way, you wouldn't ever leave the apartment let alone put on pants." She gestured with her head to my lower half.

Before I could respond, Aly came out of the back room. Her eyes were puffy and her face blotchy, and she ducked her head down as soon as she saw me.

"Jade," she chastised her friend. "What are you talking about out here?"

Jade shot her a teasing grin before winking at me. "Oh nothing. Just your lack of sexual appetite."

"I have plenty of appetite. That's not the kind of thing you should be talking about at work," Aly whispered sharply, her eyes darting over to me. My mouth spread into a grin at the blush that covered her face.

Jade shrugged as if it didn't bother her, "What else are we supposed to talk about? Coffee cozies?"

"I don't care what you talk about. Just not my sex life, or any kind of lack thereof." Aly snatched the box of napkins Jade had pulled out and started to viciously stuff them into their holder.

With Aly's hands otherwise distracted, I decided to do a little questioning of my own. "Aly?"

She didn't look up from abusing the napkins, so I said her name again. Still nothing. Reaching out, I placed my hand on her shoulder and gave it a shake.

Finally, she looked up long enough to snap at me, "What?"

"I wanted to ask you about . . . Jared," I said slowly, waiting for her reaction.

"What about him?" Aly grabbed another napkin holder and repeated her attack on it.

"Jade told me about what happened between you too," I paused as Aly gave Jade an evil glare, "Don't blame her. I asked."

"Fine. So you know what a sleazy sleazebag he is. What of it?" My master grabbed a rag and started rubbing the counter even though it was sparkling clean.

I had a feeling she was one of those angry cleaners. The kind that never cleaned their home until they were really pissed and then the next thing you knew even the silverware had been polished. It was good to know for the future.

*Future?* I asked myself. What future? After she makes her two final wishes, I was out of there. I didn't need to know about her little quirks. But even as I told myself this, I still noted it in the back of my mind.

I shook off my thoughts and then realized Aly was gone. I searched around the room for her and Jade pointed a finger toward the other side of the counter.

While I was thinking about her cleaning habits, Aly had grabbed the bucket and mop and was now working to get a stained mess off the floor. It was clearly old, and not likely to come up no matter how much she scrubbed. But still, she kept at it, bound and determined she was to defeat that stain.

Stepping over to her, I placed my hand on the mop, forcing her to stop. Aly's head popped up, and the look she gave me would have sent even the bravest human to their knees. Luckily, I wasn't human.

"Give it back," Aly cried out as I took the mop from her grasping hands.

"No. You're upset." I held the mop behind my back and leveled my gaze at her. "You need to talk about this. You can't keep it in forever."

"What are you talking about?" The exasperation in her voice almost made me think she really didn't know what I was talking about.

But I just had to know.

"Did Jared hurt you?" I paused, waiting for my words to sink in, but there was only confusion in her eyes. "You know, physically? Did he lay his hands on you?"

Then a shadow crossed over her face and just as suddenly it was gone. But I'd already seen it. He had touched her. Rage, like I had never felt before, overcame me. I would kill him. I'd make him wish he had never been born. Better yet!

"You can wish him gone," I said in a low voice. "I can do that for you, Aly. You don't have to suffer anymore."

Aly seemed to seriously think about it for a moment, before she shook her head and grabbed the mop from my now-relaxed arm. "No, I couldn't do that."

"But it would be so easy." I trailed after her as she went to put the mop up.

"I can solve my own problems. Thank you very much."

"I don't understand you humans. It's not weak to need help. You are just too damn proud to admit it," I called out after her.

Aly spun on her heel and snarled, "You want me to make a wish so bad? Well, you know what I wish? I wish you would just leave me the hell alone."

So I did.

# Chapter 13

## *Alysha*

THE MOMENT THE WORDS left my mouth I wished I could take them back.

*But that's what got you into this situation,* a voice in my head sneered.

"Where'd Mac go?" Jade asked. Her voice made me jump, causing the water from the bucket to slosh over the side.

"Uh, he had to go," I rushed to come up with an explanation. I couldn't just tell Jade I'd wished him to leave me alone so now he was gone. Gone for how long, though?

I hadn't meant to take my anger out on him. Jared was one of the things from my past I didn't like to talk about. I just wanted to move on with my life, but it seemed like my ex wasn't going to make it that easy.

Why come back after all this time? It'd been over a year since we'd broken up and I hadn't heard a peep from him. Why now?

The cynical part of me knew the most plausible reason was that Jared wanted money. It was always about money with him. The next big thing, he'd say.

Even if I wanted to give him any—which I didn't—I didn't have any to spare. All of my money went to school and to my savings for my shop. I was so close to finally being able to achieve my dream. I wasn't about to lose it to his greed.

My issues with Jared still didn't excuse my taking it out on Mac when he'd asked about him. Ever since Jared and I had broken up, Jade had been on me, wanting to find out what had really happened. I couldn't blame her for bringing Mac in on it. She cared about me, and it seemed like Mac did too.

*Well, maybe not anymore,* I thought sadly as I pushed the bucket of water back to the where it belonged in the back room. I sat down on an overturned milk crate and sighed.

Every problem I've had had been my own fault. Jade had said I was naive and too trusting. I'd thought I wasn't trusting enough.

As my relationship with Jared had disintegrated, I'd begun to not trust anything he said anymore. Which had crossed over into the rest of my life. I hated to admit it but I didn't completely trust Jade anymore, and she was my best friend!

I shouldn't let one person ruin the rest of my relationships. It wasn't fair to my potential boyfriends or to me. I wanted to be able to tell Jade everything again. Hell, I even wished I could jump into bed with Mac without worrying he was going to double-cross me.

Not like he would even consider going to bed with me now. Jared had once again ruined any chance I had for a decent relationship. If I even had a chance with Mac to begin with.

Shaking my head, I stood up. If my genie didn't like humans before, he really must hate them now. Which was also my fault.

"Are you going to mope back here all day or what?" Jade poked her head around the corner of the stock room.

"No, I'm coming." I followed Jade out of the back and into the front of the shop. We'd died down since Jared's little appearance and then Mac's disappearance. I would have given anything for the mindless rush of customers. I didn't want to think anymore. Thinking about Jared and Mac just depressed me.

"Hey," Jade elbowed me in the arm, "Cheer up. You have a sexy new guy. No reason to let that loser bring you down."

"Right," I said slowly, though I wasn't sure I even had a new guy anymore.

During the rest of my shift, it was as if I were standing on a ledge; one slight breeze and I would plunge over the edge. I messed up so many orders I'd be surprised if anyone came back the next day. Even worse were the sympathetic looks Jade kept shooting me. I swore if she patted me on the back one more time, I was going to scream.

Finally, five o'clock rolled around, and I could go home. As I gathered my things, I tried not to focus on the fact that Mac hadn't come back. Was he gone for good? I shook my head and decided not to worry about it. He'd come back when he felt like it.

Jade's shift ended at the same time as mine, and she walked out of the store with me. Before we could go our separate ways, she stopped me with a hand on my arm. Turning my attention to my friend, I hoped she wasn't going to give me another pep talk.

"Want to go get a drink? Maybe it'll help?" She cocked her head to the side causing her blue-and-purple hair to fan over her face. Just like me, she couldn't wait to take her hair down from the tight ponytail we were forced to wear during work.

I opened my mouth to say no, I just wanted to go home and crawl into bed to wallow, but I clamped my lips shut. Then changing my attitude, I gave her a half-hearted smile. "Sure. Sounds great. The usual place?"

"Say eight thirty?" Jade responded. The relief on her face made me feel bad for even considering saying no.

"Sounds good." I nodded. We said our goodbye's and went our separate ways.

When I arrived home I half expected Mac to be waiting for me, but the apartment was dark, and there was no sign of anyone being there. Disheartened, I sighed, as I sat my bag and keys down and proceeded to take my shoes off.

Digging through my pile of clean clothes, I searched for something appropriate to wear to meet Jade. I didn't drink often, but when I did it was usually with Jade. On more than one occasion I had wondered if she was a bad influence on me. Then I remembered, if it hadn't been for her, I'd be overworked more than I already was. She might be the more immature of the two of us, but at least she wasn't always stressed out.

I pulled out an olive shift dress with cut-out shoulders. It was one of my favorite outfits, and tonight I wanted to feel pretty. Laying it on the bed, I dug through my shoes until I found a pair of strappy sandals to match.

Glancing at the clock, I was relieved to see I still had over an hour until I needed to meet Jade. It wouldn't take me that long to get ready, even with taking a shower. I needed something to keep my mind from wandering to my missing genie.

So, for the first time in a long time. I cleaned my apartment.

First, the books. The pile had grown to epic proportions, so much so I didn't even know where some of them had come from. I made a pile of school books and then one of library books that needed to go back. Then I started on my clothes.

Those were a whole different story.

I admitted I was not the neatest of people, and I had let my home get a bit out of control. There were clothes from last winter in the pile of clean clothes. Obviously, I hadn't put anything up for a while. Pushing up imaginary sleeves, I began to work on putting the clean clothes in the closet. By the time that was done, it was six forty-five, and I had to hustle to get in the shower to meet Jade on time.

I didn't have too much time to spend on my makeup, so I applied mascara and some lip gloss. I dried my hair with a towel and ran some mousse through it so it wouldn't frizz out. With my top half done, I quickly donned my dress and shoes, hopping on one foot to hook the strap as I rushed out the door.

Our usual place to meet for drinks was the only bar in town: Alinity Bar and Grill. Not the most creative of names, but they didn't have any other competition so I could see why the owner didn't bother making up a better name.

Located near the college, the bar was usually packed with students. Since it was a weekday, I hoped it wouldn't be as crowded but as I approached the establishment that wish went unfulfilled. People filled the sidewalk waiting to get in, and the windows revealed the inside was just as full.

"Aly!" Jade called from the line, waving a hand above her head. She stood with a few other people who I recognized as students from Jade's art classes.

As I approached them, I saw Gregory, Jade's on-again-off-again beau, was with her too. Great. I tried not to roll my eyes and forced a smile on my face. "Hey, guys."

"Guys, this is Aly." Jade gestured to me with one hand, the other wrapped around Gregory's waist. "Aly, this is Nate and Will." She pointed to each guy in turn.

Nate was about my height with red hair and glasses. He gave me a shy smile but didn't look at me for long. Will, on the other hand, had an arrogant smirk and crooked teeth. With hair buzzed close to his head, he was definitely the less attractive of the two, but clearly the more outgoing.

"Hi." I nodded and then crossed my arms over my chest as I shot Jade a questioning look.

Seeing my look, Jade quickly explained, "I told Gregory we were going out tonight and he just happened to be going with the guys. So, I thought what the hell, let's make a night of it."

Jade's explanation didn't make me feel better. I thought it would just be the two of us. Now, I had to pretend to be interested in Gregory's friends, and that wasn't something I was equipped to deal with tonight.

It took half an hour to get into the bar and then another ten to find a table. Nate held out my chair for me and then Will plopped down in the only vacant seat next to me forcing Nate to sit between Will and Gregory. We ordered our drinks and then settled in for the next few hours.

"So, you're a business student," Will began, and then when I nodded, snorted in disdain, "That sounds boring."

Frowning, my eyes narrowed. "It's not if that's what you are into. I'd think finger painting would be boring."

Will's face scrunched up in anger. "Excuse me, I do not finger paint. I'm a sculptor. An artist. Much better than what you plan to be. An accountant?" He raised a condescending eyebrow.

Before I could answer, our drinks arrived. I thanked the waitress and took my mixed drink. I downed it pretty quickly, barely tasted the alcohol as it burned all the way down. Before she could take off, I asked the waitress for another.

"Don't you think you should slow down?" Jade placed a hand on my arm with a frown.

Shaking my head, I said, "You wanted me to have fun. So, I'm having fun. And you," I pointed a finger at Will, "for your information, I'm not going to be an accountant. I'm a baker and a damn good one." I giggled the last bit, already feeling the effects of my drink.

Will shot a questioning look at Jade who shrugged. When the waitress brought me my next drink, I felt eyes on my back. I twisted around in my seat and searched the room but didn't see anyone staring at me. Shrugging it off, I started on my next drink, this time a bit slower.

By the time we left the bar, I was stumbling over myself, and Jade had to help me walk. We made it to my apartment somehow, but when we got there, I leaned against the wall, my head heavy. I could hear Jade's voice; she was talking to someone, and I wondered who it could be, but my eyelids wouldn't stay open any longer, and I sank down onto the floor.

# CHAPTER 14
## *Mac*

TECHNICALLY, I DID GRANT Aly's wish. I stayed away but only so far that she couldn't see me. I couldn't leave her completely, no matter what she wished. Not until she made her final wish.

I would be lying if I didn't say her wish had hurt. I thought we were getting along well. Beside the fact that I had originally planned on seducing her just to get out of there, I found myself wanting to be with her. So, I followed her.

I watched from across the street, glamoured as a normal-looking fellow; one of the few abilities I was able to use outside of wish granting. Why it wasn't included in the rules, I didn't know. Maybe to protect myself from being seen? Either way, I didn't like to think much about it, in case suddenly I couldn't do it anymore.

When Aly went home, I waited outside her building. I might have been able to glamour myself, but I didn't think Aly would just ignore a random person coming into her home. It took several mind-numbing hours before she finally exited the building and it took everything in me not to drag her back into the apartment.

She was stunning. I'd never seen her this way before. While she looked great in anything, she had really put an effort in her appearance. I wished she had dressed for me and not to go out with Jade.

Following after her at a safe distance, I admired the way her dress hugged her backside and emphasised the long length of her legs. I remembered what it felt like to have those legs wrapped around me. I hoped to have them doing so again very soon.

The place Aly and Jade were meeting at was a small establishment but was already bustling with patrons. A long line trailed out of the door, and I watched with growing interest as Aly approached Jade. But Jade wasn't alone.

The man with his arm wrapped around Jade's waist had to be her beau Gregory, but the other two were clearly unattached. Their eyes roamed Aly's form with appreciation. The redhead had the decency to keep to himself, but the other one blatantly came on to Aly, making me see red. I wanted to step in to tell him . . .What exactly? I had no claim on her. Sure, we'd kissed and then some, but I was just a genie. He, like her, was human.

So I stood by and watched as the almost-balding man leered at Aly, as he took the seat next to her before the other man could, and then proceeded to insult Aly's profession.

I'd taken a table a few feet away, so I could still hear what was going on without getting caught. But I must have been staring too hard because Aly had almost caught me. I used my magic to glamour the table, so the waitress didn't bother me. Instead of a single person seated and not drinking, she thought it was full of females all with full drinks. She'd brush it off as them being slow drinkers.

By the time Aly and her friends were prepared to leave I was ready to fall asleep. I didn't know humans could drink so much. It was no wonder so many of them died young. I shook my head and followed after Jade as she tried to get an intoxicated Aly back to her apartment.

I'd almost had to intervene as the blue-haired woman tried to get Aly up the stairs. Aly was a tired drunk and kept almost knocking Jade on her ass. I wondered, not for the first time, where the men were. They should have been helping Jade get Aly home, but when Jade had said as much, they made their excuses and headed in the other direction.

*Lazy bastards.*

When Jade reached Aly's apartment, I decided I'd hidden for long enough. I materialized inside her apartment and opened the door just as Jade put the key in the door. Jade's worried expression changed to relief as soon as she saw me in the doorway.

"Thank God," she exclaimed and shoved Aly's bag and keys at me, "I forgot how much of a lightweight she is." Jade glanced down at Aly where she had passed out against the wall beside the door.

"Don't worry. I'll take care of her." I moved into the hallway and gathered Aly up in my arms. She barely weighed anything, and I found it funny that Jade had had such a hard time with her.

"I think I should stay," Jade said after a moment, coming into the apartment behind me. I shrugged and let her do what she wanted while I took Aly over to her bed.

Pulling the covers back, I laid her down gently. Maneuvering her shoes proved to be a challenge and earned me a grumbled curse from a drunken Aly, which made me smile. I slipped her leg beneath the blanket and covered her up. Immediately, she turned over and curled into a ball. I ached to wrap myself around her but remembered we weren't alone.

Moving away from the bed, I turned to Jade who was looking around the apartment in awe. "She cleaned."

Glancing around I saw what she was talking about. The books had been picked up and placed in neat piles. The clothes that had littered the ground were stacked in a basket, or up in the open closet. Seeing it made me sad. If she had been upset enough to clean so thoroughly, she must have really been hurting, and I hadn't been there for her.

*She didn't want you there,* a voice in my head said. I pushed it aside and said, "Did you need something else?"

Jade shot a look at Aly snoring away in the bed, and then suspicion filled her gaze. "Are you even supposed to be here? Where were you before?"

I rubbed the back of my neck and made something up on the spot. "I had family business to attend to so I couldn't go out with you guys."

"Then what are you doing here now?" She pointed an accusatory finger at me.

I dug into my pocket and pulled out the spare key Aly had given me before. "I have a key. Obviously, Aly doesn't mind if I'm here."

Lips pressed together in a thin line, Jade nodded. "Fine, I'm taking your word for it. But you'd better not try anything. She's vulnerable right now, and doesn't need you horn dogging on her."

I couldn't help but smile at her description. "Don't worry, I won't touch her. I'll just sleep on the couch in case she needs anything. Then I'll be gone in the morning."

"If you say so." Jade walked over to the apartment door but paused at it. "You better be good to her. She's been hurt too much already."

I didn't give her a response because whatever I said might end up being a lie. I probably wasn't good for her. In fact, I knew I wasn't. We weren't even the same species, and once she made her last wish, I wouldn't see her again.

After Jade left, I did exactly as I'd promised. Though I hated it, I laid down on the lumpy couch and tried to get some sleep.

About halfway through the night, I was awakened by Aly throwing up over the side of her bed. My nose crinkled in disgust, but I went to the bathroom and retrieved a wet washcloth and a towel.

I tossed the towel on the floor over the vomit and then sat on the bed. I held the washcloth out to her. She looked at it, and then her head moved up until it was aimed at me.

"Mac?" she croaked.

"Yes, it's me," I answered and thrust the washcloth into her hand. She took it, her expression filled with gratitude, and I went to fetch her a glass of water. Glass in hand, I sat next to her on the bed. Switching out the washcloth for the water, I lifted her hair to cool off the back of her neck. An old trick I'd learned from one of my masters; a doctor and very good at what he did.

We sat there in the dimly lit apartment while Aly drank from the glass. I took the silence as a good sign. She didn't yell at me to leave, or demand to know what I was doing there. It was possible that she was just too sick to bother with me.

"I thought you weren't coming back," Aly said after a moment.

"Sadly, no matter how much you wish it I won't leave until you make your final wish." While saying the words, I realized how much I didn't want to leave. I wanted to stay by Aly's side. No matter what that meant for me and my kingdom.

"I'm sorry about what I said. I didn't mean it." Aly put her hand on my arm, and I placed mine on top of hers and squeezed.

"I know you didn't." We were quiet again, and before it could become awkward, I stood from the bed and started back over to the couch.

"Mac," Aly's voice stopped me.

"Yeah?"

"Why don't you sleep on the bed with me?" The question hung in the air between us. I knew what it meant to humans if I shared a bed with her but did she really mean it?

At my hesitation, Aly added quickly, "Just to sleep. I don't think anyone would want to kiss me right now."

I chuckled and moved over to the other side of the bed. "I don't know about that. Having partaken in such an activity, I think many would be willing to look past the bad breath."

Giving a small giggle, Aly lay back down next to me. We remained that way for a few minutes each on our own side of the bed. Then Aly surprised me by moving over to my side. She placed an arm over my chest and one leg entangled with my own.

"Just sleeping. Got it?" She pointed a finger at me.

"Understood." I wrapped a hand around her, and she snuggled into the crook of my arm. Closing my eyes, I listened to her breathing, and the scent of her hair filled my nose. As I drifted to sleep, I thought, *I could get used to this.*

# CHAPTER 15
## *Alysha*

I WAS NEVER DRINKING again. Which was what I always said every time I drank. I usually do pretty well about keeping to that promise, but then eventually I have a shit day like yesterday, and it happens all over again. The difference between all those times and last night though was the warm muscular chest I was cuddled against.

I blinked and opened my eyes to find the sun shining into the room. Thankfully, I didn't have to work today, or I'd have been in trouble for not setting my alarm. I did have class though.

Letting out a sigh, I glanced up at my pillow who was still fast asleep. His long dark lashes brushed against the top of his cheeks as he breathed in and out. His nose was strong, almost aristocratic. Which made sense now that I knew he was a prince. My gaze fell to his lips.

I'd never been so attracted to someone's lips before. They were just the right size; not too puffy or too thin. And when he kissed me.... I let out a dreamy sigh, which turned into a groan. I needed to get to class soon.

Reluctantly rolling over in bed, I checked the clock. Just after nine o'clock. I was surprised I'd slept that long. Usually, I had to be up before seven. Sleeping in wasn't like me. Then again, I'd never had such a comfortable bed partner to give me a reason to.

Trying not to wake Mac up, I inched out of bed. I watched his face as my foot came off the bed only to land on a wet towel. A squishing sound made me grimace, and I jumped to the side. Suddenly, last night flashed back at me.

I'd gotten sick. Worst yet, I'd gotten sick in front of Mac. Embarrassment filled me, and I rubbed my hands across my face. Then I remembered how Mac had taken care of me. Even after I had been horrible to him, he had helped me clean up and probably had even been the one to put me to bed in the first place.

Smiling down at the sleeping genie, my heart swelled. How could I ever let someone like him go? I realized then that I couldn't. Which also meant, I could never make my last wish.

Guilt ate at me. I couldn't do that. If I didn't make my wish, then Mac couldn't go home.

Could I force him to stay here with me if he really wanted to be somewhere else? No. It wasn't right.

Problem was, if I made the wish I might never see him again. The thought of that made my eyes burn. It'd only been a few short days, and already I was attached to him. And we hadn't even had sex yet!

I quickly cleaned up the mess from last night, trying not to wake Mac. Then I made my way to the bathroom for a much-needed shower. So much for keeping him at arm's length. It seemed the universe was bound and determined to make me fall in love with Mac.

Love? I stopped in front of the bathroom mirror and stared at myself. Was I in love with Mac already? Wasn't it too soon?

I'd heard of people clicking right away, and I'd even heard of love at first sight, but I'd never believed in it. Never imagined it'd happen to me.

Well, it hadn't really. A voice reminded me. True enough, Mac had hated me at first, and I hadn't had any warm and fuzzies for him then either. I'd been too focused on not getting fired. Now, though, I peeked out of the bathroom at Mac, who was still asleep on the bed. Now, I couldn't imagine ever giving him up.

*But how did I make him want to stay?* I asked myself as I turned on the shower. *I couldn't.* I was finally able to answer myself. *If he wanted to stay, he'd stay on his own, but I couldn't force him.*

I heard a groan and then the sounds of movement from the other room. I quickly washed up and jumped out of the shower. Drying off, I paused at the door, I realized I hadn't grabbed any clothes.

Chewing on my lip, I then decided what the hell. It would only be a big deal if I behaved as if it was.

Opening the door as if I didn't know he was awake, I marched across the room covered in just a towel, and walked into my closet. I thanked my lucky stars that I had cleaned yesterday. It was easy enough to find something to wear and head back to the bathroom without once looking over at Mac, though I could feel his eyes burning into my skin.

With the bathroom door closed behind me, I pulled on a pair of jeans and a long-sleeved black-and-gray striped shirt. Not bothering to dry my hair, I put it up in a hair tie and then I was ready.

I made my way out of the bathroom, this time almost running into Mac.

"Woah," he said as he grabbed hold of my arms.

"Sorry about that," I muttered and then added at the last moment, "And thanks for, you know, last night."

Mac stared down at me confusion on his face. "Don't worry about it."

"I've got to get to class, and then I have to head over to work to pick up my check," I talked animatedly with my hands, trying not to look at him too long. "If you want I can come back by here first, and we can go get lunch afterward?"

I took a deep breath as I finished talking and glanced up at him. He watched me intently as if trying to decipher my intentions. Then after a moment, he seemed to have given up.

"That sounds acceptable. Do you want me to walk you to class?" he asked, a hopefulness in his voice.

I shook my head. "No, it's alright. I wouldn't want you to have to walk all the way back here."

"I don't mind," he tried again, taking a step toward me. I countered by stepping backward. Distance was good. I didn't know where we stood yet, so best not to get too comfortable. Cuddling while I was sick was one thing, but if I let myself get too used to it, I'd just end up hurt.

"It's fine. I'm running behind anyway," I declined again. "You go take a shower, and I'll see you in a few hours."

"Alright," Mac drew out, clearly not happy with my answer, but I was already headed to the door.

I opened the door and almost walk into Mac again. "Wait. Weren't you just?" I twisted around to look back into the room. I'd just left him there.

And now he was right in front of me. Scowling, I said, "What are you doing?"

"Something's wrong."

His words made my blood freeze. He knew! And then I chastised myself. He didn't know. How could he? I'd just figured it out myself.

"I don't know what you mean," I said, trying to play it cool, "But I've got to get to class, so if you would excuse me."

I pushed by him, but he caught my arm, "There's something different about you today." His eyes searched my face. It felt as if he were peering into my soul, and my face grew hot.

"Nothing's different. I'm the same old Aly," I tried to reassure him, slipping my arm out of his grasp. "I'll see you later okay?"

"Alright," Mac said finally, though the frown on his face said differently.

Before he could stop me again, I raced from the apartment. I didn't slow down until I had reached the school, and even then, I was moving faster than the rest of the students.

I tried my best to pay attention. I really did. But all the words seemed to mix together, my mind so focused on the genie back home. He suspected something, and I couldn't keep dodging him forever.

*If you made your wish it wouldn't be forever,* a voice reminded me.

I shoved the voice down. I wasn't going to make my last wish until I knew where I stood with Mac. But the only way to find that out was to tell him how I felt. The thought made my stomach twist.

Suddenly, Jade's voice filled my head. "Nothing good ever came from waiting on the sidelines. If you see something you want, you have to take it, or someone else will."

Of course, she had said those words to me when referring to my bakery, but I felt like they still applied here. She had been right then and she was right now. If I wanted Mac, I had to tell him, no matter what he said in return.

After class, I decided to pick up my check first and then grab Mac. I need to figure out what I wanted to say to him.

When I got to the coffee shop, Bruce was back and on crutches. He was fighting with Lisa, the assistant manager. Luckily, there weren't many customers to witness their display but enough that I was sure it would be around the town in no time. Nothing was secret in a small town like ours.

Lisa was the polar opposite of Bruce. Where he was tall, she was short. His skin pale, hers darker than the coffee we sold. There was not a thing about them that matched up, except maybe their souls. Which I was sure were both pitch black.

"You never spend time with me. All you care about is this stupid shop," Lisa yelled at Bruce, throwing a paper cup at him.

"This is my job, and yours," Bruce snapped back as he batted the cup to the side. "I can't just drop everything because you want to go on vacation. I'm lucky to have employees who do a good job, or I'd be screwed with this leg."

Lisa snorted and crossed her arms over her chest. "They don't deserve this place. They leech off of you, and you just let them. You're a pathetic piece of sh—"

I cleared my throat, and Lisa stopped midsentence. Her eyes narrowed, but she didn't acknowledge me. She shot Bruce a dirty look before stomping toward the office in the back.

Bruce sighed, and for the first time, I felt bad for him. No one deserved to be treated the way she had been yelling at him. Bruce might be a lot of things, but pathetic wasn't one of them.

"Hey Alysha," Bruce maneuvered over to the cash register on his crutches, "I'm assuming you are here for your check?"

"If you wouldn't mind." I pressed my fingertips together and rocked on my heels. Trying not to seem in a rush, I forced myself to wait patiently as he unlocked the register, where our checks were usually stored. I really didn't want Bruce to take his anger out on me.

"Here you go." Bruce handed me my check without much more of a look.

"Thanks." I took the envelope and spun on my heel to leave but stopped. Turning back to the counter, I asked, "How are you doing, Bruce?"

Bruce's eyes widened in a surprise, and then he seemed older all of a sudden. It reminded me that he was quite a bit older than me, though how old I wasn't sure.

"In pain but getting better," Bruce answered, and then gave me a tight smile, "Thanks for asking."

"No problem, boss." I mock saluted as I backed out of the shop.

With a smile on my face, I turned toward my apartment. Unfortunately, I didn't get more than a few feet before I was grabbed by the arm and yanked into the alley beside the shop.

"Hey babe," Jared said with a nasty smile, "It's time we had that talk."

# CHAPTER 16
## *Mac*

I KNEW THE MOMENT she awakened, but I didn't move from the bed. Instead, I watched her beneath cracked eyelids as she went about her wake-up routine as normal. I thought she might still be a bit sick after last night. And knowing her, she'd be embarrassed too.

When she went into the bathroom, it was my chance to get up. I'd hoped things between us would have been better. Aly seemed to have gotten over the encounter with Jared and her irritation with me. But then she'd started acting evasive.

She was hiding something. I didn't know what, but I knew her tells well enough now to know when she was lying. And Aly was lying through her teeth. It frustrated me to no end that I couldn't get her to admit it.

*Oh well, she would tell me when she was ready*, I reassured myself.

Waiting around today was worse than the first day. I couldn't stand the not knowing. I tried to watch television, but nothing kept me interested. The clock moved too slowly, and I wished for once I could use my full powers and not the restrained version that came with being a genie.

I smiled at the thought. What would Aly think of the real me? Not the deluded genie version, but the full one: Prince of Tavokia. Ability to pop anywhere I wanted, materializing objects out of thin air, and even transforming into other beings, not just glamouring myself to look like them.

I realized then that I wanted to show her. I needed her to know everything there was to know about me. Even—maybe if she allowed me to—take her to visit my world. I wouldn't be the first Tavokian to bring a human to our realm. There were plenty who had cross-bred which was one of the things I had wanted to put a stop to. Now, though, I couldn't even remember why.

I glanced up at the clock again and saw it had been a few hours since Aly had left. She should be getting out of class now. Since Aly had indicated we would have lunch together, I decided to jump into the shower.

While in the shower, I realized that I didn't have any other clothes to wear. I'd worn the clothes Aly had left me yesterday and hadn't seen any other suitable garments laid out for me. I climbed out of the shower and grabbed a towel, quickly drying off as I moved into the main room.

I searched the room for the clothes I had worn the first day and found them in the basket of dirty clothes. Picking up my shirt, I sniffed it and grimaced. Couldn't wear that.

Suddenly, my eyes locked onto the smaller washer and dryer system in the kitchen. I'd never used one before, but I couldn't imagine it was that hard. With a smirk, I picked up the basket of laundry and took it into the kitchen.

As it turned out, using the washer was a lot harder than it looked. I wasn't sure how much soap to put in and had ended up using too much. Which resulted in suds overflowing out the side of the machine. I quickly stopped the cycle and glared down into the top.

"Argh," I growled, grabbing my shirt and pants out of the washer and threw them into the sink. At this rate, I wouldn't be ready in time.

I used the sink water to rinse my clothes out the best I could before throwing them into the dryer. I needed it dried quickly so set it to 'Quick Dry'. Which apparently wasn't good enough for soaking wet jeans. When the timer went off, I pulled out damp jeans and a semi-dry shirt.

Frowning in dismay, I contemplated putting them back in when I felt it. A sharp pain in my chest almost knocked me off my feet. Aly.

One of the positives about being a genie was the bond between master and servant. It alerted me when they were in trouble and also enabled me to get to them at a second's notice. In case, they needed me to use a wish.

I used to be bitter about it, but now the pain only worried me. I pushed aside the discomfort of wearing wet clothing, shoved my legs into the pants and jerked my shirt over my head. I'd barely put on my shoes when I dematerialized and reappeared on the street across from Coffee and Stuff.

I searched the street and didn't see Aly anywhere. Glancing through the shop's window, I saw that her boss, Bruce, was back at work. On crutches but working. But Aly wasn't.

I was about to use my magic to find her when a scream rang out from behind the shop. I ran around the store, and my heart stopped in my chest. Jared had Aly pressed against the wall of the shop, her arm twisted behind her back.

"You always do this to me, babe," Jared growled as he pushed against her arm causing her to cry out in pain, "You should know by now that I always get what I want. Just give me the money, and I'll be out of your hair."

"Never," she snarled and then screamed as he shoved her away from the wall, throwing her to the ground. Something fluttered between them, but before Aly could grab it, Jared snatched it out of the air.

"What's this?" Jared ripped the envelope open just as I came up to them. "Your paycheck? Man, you don't get paid shit," Jared chortled, but he choked on it when he saw me. "You stay out of this. It's none of your business."

"I think it is." I glared, my anger barely contained. My gaze moved to Aly, and my eyes softened. "Are you okay?"

Swallowing, Aly licked her lips and started to get off the ground. "I'm fine."

"Good." I nodded to her and then curled my fingers into a fist and slammed it into the side of Jared's face. He went down without a fight. For how much he talked, he sure didn't have anything to back it up.

With Jared groaning on the ground, I went to Aly. Looking her over for any other injuries, I frowned. She was holding her arm gingerly and wouldn't let me touch it.

Rage roared through me, and I spun on my heel, fully intent on teaching Jared a lesson he'd never forget. Before I could get to him, Aly grabbed my arm.

Shaking her head, Aly glared down at Jared. "He's not worth it. Let's just go."

"But he was hurting you. We can't just let him get away with it." My eyes locked onto the whimpering man.

"Yes, we can," Aly pulled at me once more, "The cops can deal with him."

"Fine." I begrudgingly let her lead me away from him.

"That's right, asshole," Jared yelled after us. "Do what the bitch tells you to."

I spun on my heel so fast I feared I might get whiplash. I planned on beating him until he pleaded for mercy, but Aly got to him first.

Kicking out, she hit Jared right under the chin knocking him out cold. "I hope you rot," she snarled at his prone form. She reached out and grabbed the paper he had taken from her before. "And this is my money. Mine!"

She lifted her leg, and I assumed she was going to kick him again, but before she could, I wrapped my arms around her waist. Sirens blared in the distance, so instead of trying to drag her out of the alley, I used my magic to dematerialize us.

We reappeared at her apartment with Aly struggling against me. "Let me go!"

"Not until you calm down," I said, holding her tightly to me.

"I am calm," she growled and tried to kick my shin.

"Yes, you are the epitome of cool," I remarked, the sarcasm dripping off my words. I held onto her as she fought until eventually, she wore herself out. Head hanging, she heaved a big sigh.

"Am I a bad person?" Aly asked in a small voice.

Frowning at her question, I loosened my grip on her. "Why would you ever think that?"

"Because bad stuff keeps happening to me. First, with Jared, and then with Bruce at the shop. I can't even get a loan for my dream because of the asshole."

I didn't need to ask to know what asshole she was referring to. I smoothed a hand down her hair and held her close. "Sometimes bad things happen to good people. But it's what you do when those kinds of things happen that makes you a good person."

Aly tipped her head up to meet my eyes. "You mean how I almost kicked Jared even though he was already down?"

I smiled slightly. "Even good people have weak moments. You were justified in your anger. No one would have blamed you if you had beaten him to a pulp. Or believed him if he reported you for that matter."

Frowning, Aly pressed her cheek to my chest. "Yeah, I guess you're right. Still, you'd think being worthy enough to have a genie, I'd have better luck."

I pressed my lips together tightly and then said something I knew I would regret. "You still have one more wish left. You could change your luck around."

Aly's head jerked back, and she stared at me. "Is that what you want?"

Surprised by her question, I didn't know what to say. Was she asking me if I wanted to leave? Did she want me to leave?

"Only if that's what you want." I leaned down and pressed my forehead to hers.

I breathed her in, my heart pounding in my chest. I couldn't remember the last time I had been so nervous. I didn't know what I wanted her to say. If she wanted me to go, then I would, but then if she wanted me to stay I didn't know how we would work out. I wasn't human and would live longer than she ever would. Which was only one of the problems we would face.

I didn't get to go over any more of my hang-ups because Aly said in a quiet voice, "I think I could deal with having a bit of bad luck."

My lips spread out into a grin. I lifted her into the air, spinning in a circle while she laughed. "Really? Are you sure?"

"Yes, I'm sure." She held onto me tightly as I brought her to her feet.

Holding her about the waist, I bumped my head against hers. "Well, it looks like I'm staying. There's only one problem though."

"What's that?" Aly asked, her brow furrowing.

"I think we are going to have to buy me more than one set of clothes," I gestured to the soap still bubbling on the washer, "And you might need to show me how to actually wash my clothes.”

Placing a hand over her mouth, Aly laughed, “I think I can help you out with that. After all, I just got paid.” She held up the envelope she had retrieved from Jared.

“Well, I don’t know about you,” I started to lower my head, “But I’m starving.” But not for food, I finished internally as I took hold of her mouth with mine.

# CHAPTER 17
## *Mac*

WHEN I WOKE UP the next morning, I was feeling particularly good about myself. I mean, I had just had the best sex of my long life. Of course, I'd be happy. Even more so because it was with someone I cared for so deeply.

I rolled over and reached for Aly, intent on rekindling last night's activities, but my hand found an empty bed. Frowning, I sat up and opened my eyes. The room was filled with light, and the clock told me it was after eleven.

*Had she said she had to work today?*

I eased out of bed, not bothering to get dressed. My back ached, and I smiled in memory. Who knew Aly was such a hellcat? She'd sure given me a run for my money.

Going to the kitchen, I poured myself a glass of water and thought about stopping by the coffee shop to see her. If she was there, waiting until this afternoon to see her again, to touch her once more, would be torture. I wanted her now.

Setting my glass in the sink, I moved over to where a pile of clothing sat for me. Deja vu. Hadn't she done this once before? The note on top of the clothes told me she had cleaned them before she went to the bank. She'd be back in a few hours.

Well, at least I wouldn't have to wait until this afternoon to see her again, though, I wasn't sure when she had written the note. It could have been hours ago or even minutes ago. I had no idea when she'd be back.

Once again, I found myself having to entertain myself. If I was going to stay in the human world with her, I needed to find something to do with myself. I couldn't just let Aly pay for everything. I was supposed to take care of her, not the other way around.

I would need to get a job. Though, how I would go about doing that with no identification or credentials, I didn't know. But I was sure Aly could help me figure it out.

Setting the note back on the counter, I gathered up the clothes and went to the bathroom. While I was washing up, the front door to the apartment opened. I hurried out of the shower, excitement filling me to see Aly again.

Before I could get out of the bathroom to greet Aly, a body appeared in front of me and blocked my path. My cousin, Ga'nova, stood in front of me. Dark-haired like me, he was older by a few centuries and had piercing green eyes. He was dressed in the casual clothing from Tavokia, slacks, and an open-neck shirt, he glanced around the tiny bathroom with disdain.

"Hello, cousin," he said when his gaze finally landed on me. "You are looking well." Ga'nova drew out as his eyes raked over my nude appearance.

"What are you doing here?" I demanded, trying to keep my voice low. I didn't want Aly to hear and come barging in. If my cousin was here, then nothing good would come of it.

"I heard from a little birdy that you were about to break the spell," he smirked at me, "and I just wanted to make sure you were sure you knew what you were doing."

Aly's voice could be heard through the bathroom door as she called my name. I didn't answer her. I glared at Ga'nova to remain quiet. For once, my cousin listened and kept his mouth closed until Aly's phone went off and she walked away from the door to answer it.

"I'm going to ask you one more time, Ga'nova," I pointed a finger at my cousin's chest, "What are you doing here? Did you just come to make sure

I wouldn't break the spell? Because I'll have you know I have no intentions of breaking it."

Ga'nova cocked a brow. "Not even if it's what your master wants?"

"But she doesn't," I argued. "We already talked about it. She doesn't want me to leave."

"But aren't you being selfish?" Ga'nova asked a pitying look on his face. "You were sent to her for a reason."

"And what reason is that?" I spat back at him.

"To make her dreams come true of course, and by not granting her wish you are not doing your duty." My cousin's chastising tone made me frown.

I hadn't been lying when I had told Aly she'd only received my bottle because she deserved it. Just like all my other masters, though, I had done my best to not give any of them what they really wanted. The same went with Aly. But what if Ga'nova was right? What if I was the reason Aly would never get her bakery?

I couldn't live with that. The guilt would eat me alive.

"There has to be another way." I shook my head and then stared at the bathroom door as if I could see Aly through it.

"You know our people have some gifts of foresight, which was put into the spell. You would go to those worthy of your gift. Those who would have never achieved it without some kind of magical intervention." He turned the knob of the bathroom door before I could stop him, cracking it open enough for me to hear Aly's conversation.

She was talking to Jade. The bank hadn't gone well. I closed my eyes briefly as she said the words I wished I would never hear from her.

"You know what you have to do," Ga'nova urged, and when I tried to go out to the front room he stopped me with his hand. "You can't grant it in front of her. Especially not like that." He pointed down to my unclothed form.

"Why not? She's seen me like this before." I didn't see what the big deal was and I wanted to hold her, kiss her one more time before I was sent back to my world.

"There's a little stipulation in your spell. One that I came here to tell you about." He gave me a smug smile that made me want to punch him in the face.

"Well, spit it out why don't you." My fingers curled into a fist, the desire to hit him almost overwhelming.

"If you grant this wish, as you should, your spell will be broken, and you'll return home to your kingdom, but..." he held up a finger to emphasize his point, "It will also make her and all your previous masters forget you ever existed. They will think they just had a spot of good luck."

My stomach sank. That was something I hadn't known. I'd thought I could make her dream come true, go home to take care of some things, and then come back to pick up where we'd left off. But if she didn't remember me, I couldn't even see her beforehand. The moment I granted it, she'd forget about me. I could see how a naked stranger in her home would not be a good idea.

"I can't do it." I looked to Ga'nova who nodded his head in agreement.

"I can see this is a hard decision. I wouldn't want to make it any more difficult for you, so feel free to take your time. But a chance like this might not come again. She may never make a wish like that again," his gaze settled on me, his lips pressed into a thin line. "Can you deal with that?"

Before I could answer, Ga'nova disappeared. I quietly closed the bathroom door and leaned against it. He was right. Of course, he was right. He'd always been the more responsible one. But just thinking of Aly not remembering me made my heart break. How could I give her what she wanted more than anything in the world and then lose her like that?

I turned around and placed my forehead against the cool surface of the bathroom door. I could hear her voice just through the the wood, and I wanted so badly to go out there and see her. But I knew I couldn't.

If I saw her, I wouldn't do what needed to be done. I couldn't be selfish. If I loved her, I had to give her what she deserved. Even if it meant she wouldn't remember me.

I closed my eyes and brought her face to the forefront of my mind. With a slight push of magic, I granted my very last wish as a genie.

# Chapter 18

## *Alysha*

I COULD KILL THE guy at the bank. Seriously, could he have been any more prejudiced? Sure, I was young and yes, maybe I didn't exactly look like a responsible business owner, but that didn't mean I wouldn't be one.

I threw my keys onto the side table by the door. I immediately searched for Mac, but he wasn't in the main room, and the bathroom door was closed.

Maybe he was going to the bathroom? Then I wondered. Did genies even do that? There was so much about Mac that I didn't know, and now that we'd slept together I needed to clear the air between us. Find out who I really was getting into my bed with.

I started toward the bathroom, intent on knocking but my phone went off. I glanced down at the screen. Jade was calling; she'd want to know what had happened at the bank.

"Don't even ask," I said as I answered the phone. I plopped down on the couch with a tired sigh.

"Didn't go well I take it?" Jade asked, sympathy in her voice.

"The guy is such a hater. I don't think I'd ever get a loan from him unless I changed how I looked entirely, and even then, if I didn't have a husband to help me out he'd still tell me I was in over my head."

"Misogynist," Jade snarled, and I couldn't disagree. All of the employees seemed to have a twenties mindset. If I didn't have a man to stand by me, I wasn't worthy of their time. My piercings and tattoo just added to my offenses.

"I'm just so tired of being rejected," I sighed into the phone. "I just want someone to give me a chance."

"You'll get it, don't worry," Jade tried to console me. "Remember, I have a feeling."

"Yeah, yeah. I know," I interrupted her before she could go on a long tangent about her psychic abilities, "But your feeling or not, it's not happening now."

"You don't know that. It still could. Just give it time."

I drew my legs up under me and growled, "You know, I just wished for once someone would care about my dreams and ambitions and not the bottom line. I wish I could get everything I wanted without having to fight so hard for it."

"Well, you know what they say about wishes," Jade said a smile in her voice.

"Yeah well. I'm about all out of wishes," I muttered. Jade didn't know how true that statement was. I had one wish left, and I could use it to get my dream but then I'd lose Mac, and that wasn't something I was willing to trade.

"Anyways," Jade continued, "I'm in the middle of a crucial piece. Can I call you later?"

"Sure," I said half-heartedly and hung up the phone. Talking about it wasn't going to make me feel any better. If anything, it would make me feel worse.

What would make me feel better was the sexy genie who was supposed to be at my beck and call? I frowned again at Mac's absence. Where was he?

"Mac?" I called out, scanning the room even though I knew there was only one other room he could be in if he was still in the apartment. I stood from the couch and started toward the bathroom again. I only got about halfway there when I stopped for some reason.

Why was I going to the bathroom again? I didn't need to go. My head fuzzy, I had a weird feeling that I was forgetting something. Something important. Maybe I had a test?

*No. I didn't have one,* I thought after I scanned through my phone to check my calendar. What the heck was it?

Before I could think on it any longer, my phone rang. Glancing down at the caller I.D., I frowned. What was the bank calling me for? They'd already told me no for the millionth time, did they just want to drill it in more?

"Hello?" I answered, irritation in my voice.

"Alysha?" the man from the bank—Mr. Harold—asked as if unsure if he had the right number.

"This is she," I said, crossing one arm under the other holding the phone. "What can I do for you?"

"I'm glad I caught you. You see, there's been a change in your application." There was a gleefulness to his tone that bothered me. I didn't trust it.

"What could have changed in the last half hour?" I said between clenched teeth. "You made it pretty clear that I was never going to get a loan from you."

Mr. Harold cleared his throat and then stumbled over his words as he said, "That's true. I did say that. But it was a mistake. We here at Alinity Credit Union would be delighted to lend you the money to start your bakery. I've personally had the pleasure of having one of those delicious creations you make for Coffee and Stuff and think you have a real chance of succeeding."

Speechless. I was utterly speechless. I grabbed the back of the couch as my knees became weak beneath me.

"Alysha? Are you still there?" Mr. Harold asked, and I shook myself out of my stupor.

"Yes, yes. I'm still here," I quickly said before he could hang up. "So, what exactly are you saying?"

Harold sighed, frustration clear in that one breath. "I'm saying you got your loan. If you don't want it . . ."

"No! No," I said, forcing my voice back to a normal tone, "I want it. I just never dreamed I would actually get it."

"Well, believe it," Mr. Harold stated. "If you could come in on Monday to sign some papers we can get you started on finding your new shop."

I nodded, then remembered I was on the phone and he couldn't see me. "Yes, I can be in on Monday. Bright and early."

"Why don't we say ten o'clock? Gives me time to get into the office."

"Fine. Yes. Ten o'clock. I'll be there," I confirmed and then stared down at the phone after Mr. Harold said goodbye.

I'd actually done it. I was going to get the money I needed to start my own shop, and I got it all on my own. Letting out a squeal, I ran around the apartment. Jumping up and down on the bed, I couldn't contain my excitement.

"I have to call Jade," I said after a moment and got off the bed to do just that. My foot caught on something, and I almost faceplanted on the couch.

Frowning, I picked up the item I had tripped over. It was a pair of men's pants. Staring at it curiously, I wondered. *Where had these come from?*

I didn't spend much time fretting about. Figuring it was something of Jared's he'd left there, I tossed it toward my laundry basket. I missed, but I didn't bother to go pick it up. Instead, I dialed Jade's number and almost screamed into the phone.

"Jade you won't believe what happened!"

"What? Did you finally get laid?" Jade's teasing voice said back.

Scowling, I said into the phone, "No, you know I haven't been with anyone since Jared." Not letting her bring me down, I changed the subject. "I got the loan."

"What?" Jade gasped and then let out of a squeal of her own. "That's great news! See I told you I had a feeling. You didn't listen."

"Yeah, yeah. You're right. I'm wrong." I chuckled.

"Well, this means we have to celebrate. Get your butt over here. We are going to get smashed and then decide how we are going to tell Bruce to suck it."

"You got it." I laughed with her as I grabbed my keys off the side table by the door. My hip bumped against the side of it causing an ugly bottle I didn't remember buying, to fall off and break into several pieces.

I frowned down at it but then brushed it off. I'd clean it up later. Who wanted to clean on a day like this?

"I'm on my way," I told Jade as I hung up the phone. I pushed the broken glass to the side with my foot so I wouldn't step on it when I got home. Bag and keys in hand, I closed the apartment door and locked it behind me. My heart full of the future.

# CHAPTER 19
## *Mac*

LEAVING ALY HAD BEEN the hardest thing I had ever done. Even more so than when I had first become a genie. I couldn't have imagined anything else would ever compare.

The moment I'd granted Aly's wish I'd felt different. Thankfully, my powers came back in a rush allowing me to clothe myself before I started to disappear. I reappeared before the court, which was in full session at that point.

"Prince Mac'voniak you're back!" one of the older nobles, Roc'ah, cried out. He had been one of my father's advisers and seemed he still held that position with my cousin.

Roc'ah's announcement caused an uproar of mixed responses. Some of the others surrounded me, bombarding me with question after question. Ones that I couldn't even begin to answer. And others looked to my cousin, Ga'nova, who sat on the throne above everyone else.

I'd never liked him. He was too serious. Too focused on duty to ever be of any interest to me. *The past me,* I reminded myself.

"Silence!" Ga'nova called out, causing the courtroom to instantly quieten. The attention of the room turned to him as he descended from his throne. The nobles cleared a path for him as he passed by. I stood where I had appeared, not certain if I would be welcomed with a death sentence. He had been the one to try and make me stay with Aly.

I didn't have anything to fear though. Ga'nova stopped in front of me, his eyes scanning over my form. Then suddenly he clapped me on the shoulders, a broad smile covering his lips as he laughed.

"Welcome back, cousin! I knew you could do it."

"You did?" I raised a brow. I was under the impression he'd wanted me to fail.

"Of course! Who do you think gave your father the idea?" Ga'nova wrapped an arm around my shoulders and led me out of the crowd, toward the throne. "To be honest, when you took so long to break the spell I doubted you would come back. But you proved me right after all."

"Yes, I wasn't sure of myself either," I answered, still a bit cautious of his acceptance.

"Well, that's all over now. It's in the past," he waved a hand off to the side, "And now we must get you back to your proper place."

"And where would that be?" I quirked a brow at him, fully expecting him to throw me in the dungeon, or worse. I forced myself not to shudder at the thought of what could be worse in my cousin's mind.

"On the throne, of course." He frowned for a moment and then motioned to a few servants standing by. "Make sure the king's old room is prepared for Mac'voniak and start moving my things out of the main chamber. My cousin will be wanting his parents' room after all."

"Oh, you don't have to worry about that," I held my hands up, "I haven't been here in so long, I wouldn't even begin to know what is going on in the kingdom."

The moment the words came out of my mouth, Ga'nova jumped on them. "Of course, you don't and why should you? But never fear," he patted me on the back, "we will get you up to date and to ruling in no time."

Things were moving all too fast for me. Just moments ago, I'd been thinking about the future I could never have with Aly, and now I was being prepped to take over Tavokia. Sure it was what I always wanted, but things had changed. I'd changed. I wasn't sure I wanted to rule Tavokia anymore. Not if it meant I could never see Aly again.

*Not that she'd remember me anyway.*

"Ga'nova," I said, stopping my cousin as he continued to order the servants around, "Can we speak in private?" I looked to the audience of nobles, their eyes focused solely on Ga'nova and me.

"Of course, cousin." He waved a hand at the nobles to disperse, but I wasn't about to talk about this here where anyone could listen in.

"I meant more private than this." I gestured around the room. "What I have to say isn't anything you would want others to hear."

Frowning at me, Ga'nova nodded, "Very well. Let us retire to my office."

Following after my cousin, my hands became clammy. I didn't know how I was going to tell him I didn't want to rule. I just wanted to go back to the human realm. If he was the same man I knew from before, he would be delighted to stay in power. But this new version of him had me doubting he hadn't changed.

"Now, cousin," Ga'nova said taking a seat behind his desk, which had once been my father's—a large oak that spanned the width of the room. I remembered playing under it as a child while my father worked. I had always envisioned I'd be the one sitting behind it one day.

"I know," Ga'nova said, his eyes suddenly sad, "I miss him too sometimes. It was a real tragedy that he wasn't able to see you break the spell."

"Yeah," I agreed, "Too bad."

"He'd have been proud of you, you know," my cousin continued. "He always had faith you would find your way back home. Your father had such high hopes for you. Thought if you would just grow up a little, you'd be a great king and I think he was right."

"That's what I wanted to talk to you about," I started before he could keep going on about my father's praises. If he kept talking, I wasn't sure I would be able to say what I had to say. I might 'be convinced of my place here and not where my heart was.

I took a deep breath and then said, "I can't be king."

Ga'nova looked at me for a moment and then laughed, "Don't worry, nobody expects you to figure it out right away. Of course, you'll have to shadow me for a bit to figure out what is happening. You need to be brought up to date on the ogre alliance, and the dragon shifters are making demands again."

"No, Ga'nova," I cut him off, "I won't be king."

"What do you mean 'won't'?" His brows furrowed in confusion and then raised in surprise. "This is about that woman isn't it?" I opened my mouth to answer but he continued, giving me an understanding look, "I know you must have loved her, otherwise you wouldn't have been able to break the spell, but you do realize she's human and you are practically immortal. It would never work."

I shook my head. "I don't care. I can't stay here when my heart really lies with her. It wouldn't be right."

"But she doesn't even remember you," Ga'nova reminded me. "You destroyed any chances of a relationship with her when you granted her last wish."

"I'll make her remember," I insisted, running a hand through my hair. "If not, then I'll make her fall in love with me again. This time as a man not as a genie."

"I'm sorry, Mac'voniak. It's just not possible." He held his hands out to his sides. "There is no way the council is going to agree to let you go now that you are back. What is worse, they will think I had something to do with it, and I can't have that."

"Then I will make them understand." I forced all my determination, all my desperation to get back to Aly into my voice, hoping to make him understand.

Ga'nova nodded. "Very well. It is your decision after all. I can't force you to take the crown, but you have been gone a long time. There is much to catch up on before you can leave. That is if the council even lets you leave."

"Just let them try to stop me." The venom in my voice surprised even me, but I wasn't about to let a group of old men keep me from Aly. I'd die first.

It turned out the council was more than happy to let Ga'nova continue ruling. On the condition that I stayed to oversee the proper ceremonies to officially declare him the rightful ruler and that I was giving up any claim to the throne. I had no problem with any of this, but as the days turned to weeks, I became anxious to get back to Aly.

"This is taking too long," I complained to Ga'nova in his office one day after sitting through a meeting about the trolls.

"You must have patience, cousin. You will get to leave soon. I promise."

"You've been saying that for months now, and I'm no closer to leaving than I was before," I argued and then pointed at the complaint on the desk in front of him. "I'm being forced to stay here for this kind of juvenile crap?"

The trolls were complaining that the water nymphs were flooding their bridges on purpose. The nymph said the trolls were just being big babies. The water had only risen about an inch above the normal, and it was usual for the season.

Ridiculous nonsense. I didn't have time for those kinds of trivial complaints. I needed to get back to Aly.

When I wasn't in meetings, I spent time in the library, scouring every text I could on memory spells. I was determined to find something that would help trigger Aly's memory. I had finally come up on something last week, in a beaten-up old text that was barely legible. But I had deciphered it enough to figure out what I had to do.

The only way to break a memory spell like Aly's was to trigger the emotion. Whatever she felt for me would break the spell. Whether it be love or hate. I had to make her feel it again. Then, and only then, would she remember.

It couldn't be that hard. I'd made her fall for me in a few days. I had no doubt I could do it again. If I could just get to her.

"They might seem silly to you, but these are our people. We can't just ignore them 'cause we have something better to do," Ga'nova explained. "The ceremonies are done. We are just waiting for the council's final approval. Then you can flit off to your human."

"Fine. I will wait." I crossed my arms over my chest and nodded.

While I had told my cousin I would follow the rules, I had grown tired of waiting. I had a feeling they weren't going to let me leave anytime soon, and when they did it might be too late. Aly could have moved on and found someone else. Or even worse, died.

No. I couldn't wait any longer. If I was ever going to get back to her, it had to be now. If the council came after me, I'd have to deal with it later.

# CHAPTER 20
## *Alysha*

ALMOST A YEAR HAD passed since I'd finally gotten my big break. I'd thought it would never happen. That I'd forever be looking to the future, hoping and waiting for someone to give me a chance.

Then it had finally happened. I didn't know how it came about, but it did. The loan officer had already told me I didn't have enough collateral to be worth the investment, and then he suddenly changed his mind. The finance fairies were finally in my court, and now, here I was, realizing that dream.

Make a Wish Bakery was everything I had hoped it would be. No longer did I have to stare at the ugly inside of Coffee and Stuff. Instead, I had the walls painted a pale mint green; just looking at them calmed me. Jade and I had designed the uniforms, avoiding everything we'd hated about the old ones we'd been forced to wear at Bruce's shop.

The uniforms were black pants and green shirts that matched the paint on the walls. On the top right corner of each shirt was a shooting star, the company logo, and the name of the bakery. Unfortunately, we still had to keep our hair up—if we wanted to avoid facing the health inspector—but it was a small price to pay to own my own place.

"You did good, Aly," Jade said coming up beside me behind the cash register.

I smiled at her as I finished up the next customer's order. "We did a good job."

Jade's grin widened. "Yeah, I guess we did."

While I was technically the owner and boss, Jade had become my right *and* left-hand woman. She acted as assistant manager as well as the creative mind behind all our advertising efforts.

It had been her idea to put the shop next to the college. A decision that was by far the best ever. Coffee and Stuff was on the other side of town, and most students didn't have time to travel the ten minutes it took to get there. So, a shop right beside the campus had ended up being a gold mine.

No, if it hadn't been for Jade, I would never have gotten the shop off the ground. Nor where we were today, a line down the block and the ledger in the black.

I had everything I'd ever wanted, and I should have been happy. But for some reason, even as I reminded myself of that fact, a pain in my chest said something was missing. For the life of me, I couldn't figure out what it was. Shrugging it off, I continued to serve the never-ending line of customers with a genuine smile on my face.

"There's a guy staring at you," Terry—who I had convinced to leave Coffee and Stuff to work for me—said. He pointed a dark red-painted nail out the window of the shop.

I followed the direction he indicated until my eyes landed on a man standing across the street. To someone else, it might seem like he was just observing the shop, trying to decide if he wanted to come in. But just like Terry had said, the man was clearly staring at me, and when our eyes locked, he lifted a hand as if he knew me.

I lifted my hand, my brow furrowed. Maybe he was from one of my classes and I just didn't remember? No. I'd have remembered someone like him.

As I tried to figure out where I knew him from, the man made his way across the street and toward the shop. My eyes ate up his long legs, encased in form-fitting jeans, and his muscular top half displayed by his form-fitting t-shirt. He had a strong jaw and an aristocratic nose, and that pain in my chest panged.

Why couldn't I remember him?

He stood at the back of the line—that had for once stopped just inside the door. I became more anxious with each customer I helped. My heart beat faster, my palms becoming sweaty. It was as if I wanted to see this guy. I hadn't felt this way about anyone since . . .

I shook the thought off. I wouldn't let my ex ruin today for me. He was long gone. Moved to a different country as far as I knew.

"Who's the hottie?" Jade asked quietly at my elbow. I glanced at her and then back at the guy she had been referring to. Who happened to be the same man I'd been waiting on.

"Hi." my voice came out breathless for some reason, and I cleared my throat. Jade giggled, and I shot her a warning look, then turned my attention back to the man in front of me. "Welcome to Make a Wish Bakery. How can I help you?"

*There that was better*, I commended myself. I could be a normal person. He was a customer like all the others.

Except he wasn't. His dark eyes glittered with amusement, and he leaned his elbows on the waist-high counter. "I heard your place has the best coffee in town."

"Is that so?" I quipped, forcing myself not to grin like an idiot. His voice was deep and accented, though I wasn't sure from where. It had to be something Middle Eastern.

"Most definitely." He nodded, his grin broadening. "So, I just had to come over and check it out myself."

Not even paying any mind to the customers waiting behind him, I asked, "And where is that?"

"Oh, I live quite far away from here," he commented and then smirked as if it were some kind of joke. "It's another world altogether."

"Well, that sounds interesting," I drew out. His words triggered something in me. He was so familiar,."I'm sorry, this is going to sound crazy," I blushed and shook my head, "But have we met before?"

The man straightened, the expression on his face one I could only describe as hopeful. "Unfortunately, I haven't had the pleasure. I'm Mac." he held his hand out for me to shake.

I stared down at it for a moment, nervous about touching him for some reason. Then I pushed away the feeling and slid my hand into his.

The moment our hands touched, my eyes widened. Hot desire zipped through my hand and settled low in my stomach. Suddenly, everything came back. How I'd dropped the bottle in the water bucket. Mac's sudden appearance. Bruce breaking his leg. Even what had happened with Jared. Then it all ended with Mac disappearing around the same time I got my loan.

"It was you," I accused, anger filling me, "This is all because of you."

Mac didn't even try to deny it though, I could read the guilt on his face. He tried to remove his hand from mine, but I held fast. I jerked him forward and pressed my mouth to his. All the emotions I had for him came spiraling into me, and I shoved those into our kiss.

We would have stayed like that had Jade not cleared her throat behind us. Finally releasing him, I growled, "Don't you ever leave me again."

Giving me one of his panty-melting grins, Mac replied, "Never. You couldn't wish me away."

# About the Author

Erin Bedford is an otaku, recovering coffee addict, and Legend of Zelda fanatic. Her brain is so full of stories that need to be told that she must get them out or explode into a million screaming chibis. Obsessed with fairy tales and bad boys, she hasn't found a story she can't twist to match her deviant mind full of innuendos, snarky humor, and dream guys.

On the outside, she's a work from home mom and bookbinger. One the inside, she's a thirteen-year-old boy screaming to get out and tell you the pervy joke they found online. As an ex-computer programmer, she dreams of one day combining her love for writing and college credits to make the ultimate video game!

Until then, when she's not writing, Erin is devouring as many books as possible on her quest to have the biggest book gut of all time. She's written over thirty books, ranging from paranormal romance, urban fantasy, and even scifi romance.

**Come chat me up!**
www.erinbedford.com
Facebook.com/erinrbedford
twitter.com/erin_bedford
Don't forget to follow me on Goodreads, Pinterest, Instagram, and YouTube!

**Want to be the first to know about my new releases?**
Erinbedford.com/newsletter